HOT SHOT

Nutty moved back to the other end of the court. Dribbled twice. Up. Floating, watching the ball. Pop. "Nice shooting, Nutty," people were yelling. Nutty had to smile. They didn't know. They didn't understand what was happening. They didn't know the ball the way he did.

Nutty made eight straight baskets, and the score was 16 to 4 before the other coach called a time-out. Nutty didn't want to go to the side. There were too many distractions over there. And then everyone was pounding him on the back.

Nutty started to laugh. He had always wanted to be a good athlete, and now he really was. "Thanks, guys," he was saying. "I guess I'm just hot."

NUTTY CAN'T MISS

Dean Hughes

A BANTAM SKYLARK BOOK®
TORONTO • NEW YORK • LONDON • SYDNEY • AUCKLAND

RL 5, 008–012

This edition contains the complete text
of the original hardcover edition.
NOT ONE WORD HAS BEEN OMITTED.

NUTTY CAN'T MISS
A Bantam Book / published by arrangement with Atheneum Publishers

PRINTING HISTORY
Atheneum edition published April 1987

Bantam Skylark edition / April 1988

*Skylark Books is a registered trademark of Bantam Books. Registered in U.S.
Patent and Trademark Office and elsewhere.*

ISBN 0-553-15584-9

Published simultaneously in the United States and Canada

---

*Bantam Books are published by Bantam Books, a division of Bantam Double-
day Dell Publishing Group, Inc. Its trademark, consisting of the
words "Bantam Books" and the portrayal of a rooster, is Registered in U.S. Patent
and Trademark Office and in other countries. Marca Registrada.
Bantam Books. 666 Fifth Avenue, New York, New York 10103.*

PRINTED IN THE UNITED STATES OF AMERICA

S   0 9 8 7 6 5 4 3 2 1

For Bill J. Hurst, Kym, and Becky

CHAPTER ONE

Most of the boys on the team were just messing around, shooting baskets, but Nutty Nutsell and Orlando Ortega were playing a little game of one-on-one. At the moment, Orlando was bending forward, holding the ball and making head fakes to one side and then the other. "I'm going to drive past you, Nutty. I'm too quick for you."

"Just do *something*, will you?" Nutty said. The coach, Nutty's dad, was blasting away on his whistle, but no one was paying any attention.

"I'm going to make my move. And you can't stop me. Maybe left. Maybe right. You don't know which way I'm going."

"Yeah I do. You can't dribble with your left hand."

"Oh, the heck I can't." Orlando straightened up and relaxed. And then—*bam*—he drove to the left . . . and dribbled the ball off his foot.

1

Nutty was laughing, but Orlando didn't think it was so funny. "Hey, I can go to my left."

"Yeah, you can. You just can't take the ball with you."

"At least if I get a shot I can make it. You can't hit *nothing*." Orlando sounded sort of mad, and he looked mad too, with his dark hair hanging in his eyes, but Nutty knew he was just playing around.

"All right, boys," Mr. Nutsell was yelling, "come over here and sit down for a minute." He was standing with his hands on his hips, his jaw thrust forward. He had bought himself new basketball shoes, new sweats, and a genuine big-league, chrome-plated whistle.

As the guys finally walked over toward Mr. Nutsell, Nutty paused, still reacting to Orlando's smart-aleck comment about his shooting. He gave Orlando a sarcastic little smile but decided not to say anything. The truth was, he wasn't a very good shooter; but then, neither was Orlando.

Mr. Nutsell was waving for the rest of the guys to hurry. Nutty could see that he was trying to show that he planned to be firm with them. "He's going to take this coaching thing seriously," Nutty mumbled to himself. "I was afraid of that."

"Sit down in the bleachers, boys," Mr. Nutsell was saying. He pointed to places nearby.

Nutty walked up close and whispered, "Dad, please don't give any speeches, okay?"

His dad shot him a dirty look and said, "Just sit down, Freddie."

A couple of the guys laughed. No one ever called Nutty anything but Nutty. A lot of kids didn't even know what his real name was.

"All right, young men . . ." Mr. Nutsell hesitated, then nodded solemnly, looking around at the boys. He had his legs spread rather wide and his arms crossed on his chest. This was his forceful, authoritative look; Nutty had seen it before. But Mr. Nutsell was too tall and thin, and he had too many freckles: He looked more like Nutty than like the hard-nosed coach he wanted to be.

"I have called you 'young men' because that's what you are. You may only be in fifth grade, but you're growing up, and let me tell you something important: There's nothing better to make a boy a man than to participate in organized sports. To go out there on that field and give all you've got, pit your best against someone else's best—that's the great American way. It will make men out of you. I believe that with all my heart." He clapped his fist against his chest.

Nutty wanted to die. Dad was going to do it; he never could resist a chance to give a speech.

"Boys—I mean, young men—I want to start our first practice right. I want to make a couple of things clear from the very beginning. And the first thing I want you to know is that I expect every one of you to give *everything* you have—and then a little more—every minute of every practice, and every minute of every game. If you aren't ready to do that—if you can't give all you have, plus a little, all the time—I want you to tell me right now."

"We'll run out, Mr. Nutsell."

"What?"

"If we keep giving all we have, plus some extra, pretty soon we won't have any of what we've got." It was Richie Fetzer, one of Nutty's closest friends. He never took things very seriously, and being rather small and not what you would call athletic, he especially didn't take basketball seriously.

All the boys were laughing. Mr. Nutsell wasn't. "Well, now, Richie, that's the interesting thing about giving everything. The more you give, the more you have, and then you reach within yourself and you find some more, because what's there comes from the heart, and the heart never stops pumping in the chest of a real athlete." He paused and pointed a finger at Richie. "A true athlete never finds the bottom to his well of commitment, because the commitment comes from desire. And desire runs as deep as an athlete's very soul. If he doesn't have it, he's nothing, no matter how great he might seem, and if he does have it, he's everything, because nothing else matters. Can you understand that?"

Richie was shaking his head, saying he didn't understand, but Mr. Nutsell didn't notice, or chose not to. He was looking around at the other boys. Nutty thought they looked sort of confused.

Orlando was groaning. "Nutty, I told you he'd start this kind of stuff."

"And that's what I want you to be, my young friends: *real athletes, true athletes*. When all is said and done, whether you win the championship won't matter very much. But if you learn to keep going when the going gets tough, to turn challenges into opportunities, to keep your eye on the mark, to build true character so that you can get out there in that business world and really compete, then you'll—"

"Frankly, Mr. Nutsell," Charley Blackhurst said, "we've learned enough character over the last couple of years. What we want to do now is *win*." Bilbo (that's what everyone called Charley because he liked *The Hobbit* so much) was tall, and he was a pretty good player, even if he did spend more time reading than practicing basketball.

"That's right," Orlando shouted, "we want to win this year," and all the other guys shouted out their agreement.

"Well, sure. I understand that. That's something we all believe. A man has to know how to win. Winning isn't everything to us; it's the *only* thing. Let's never forget that." Somehow, Mr. Nutsell's voice lacked conviction. "But on the other hand, if we do lose, you know, we still could learn from that. That's all I'm saying. I want you boys to prepare yourselves for life, to learn the drive and guts it takes to survive out there in this dog-eat-dog world. I want you never to fear the competition and —"

"What kind of offense are we going to use?" someone asked. Nutty turned to look. It was the guy everyone called Noodle. His last name was Nodel; he was very tall, and skinny as a garden hose. He went to Reese School. There weren't many kids at the University Laboratory School, which Nutty and his friends attended, so the people who ran the city recreation league ruled that some Reese students could play for the Lab. The only trouble was, Reese always took the best athletes and then just sent over anyone else who wanted to play. This year, there were three other guys besides Noodle: a short kid named Rodney Mirkle, who could dribble okay but couldn't shoot worth a darn; a shorter guy named Peter Pandelli, who couldn't dribble too well but could shoot a little better than Mirkle; and an even shorter guy named Gary Goutz, who couldn't do anything.

They didn't inspire a lot of hope. All the same, this was a big year for all the fifth-grade guys like Nutty and his friends. This was their last chance to do well in the city league. Since Warrensburg had a middle school that started with sixth grade, the fifth graders were the oldest boys in the recreation league. If they didn't do well this year, it was all over.

"Excuse me, young man, we'll—"

"Noodle," Orlando said.

"What's that?" Mr. Nutsell sounded a little irritated. Maybe he thought he had been called a name.

"Noodle. That's his name."

"It's really John," the kid said.

"You better call him Noodle and your son Nutty," Orlando said. "If you call them John and Freddie, we won't know who you're talking about."

"Orlando, let me decide that." Nr. Nutsell was getting frustrated. Nutty could see that. "Now listen. I want you boys to be clear about something from the beginning. I'm the coach. I'm in charge. You do things my way, or you don't do them. I'm not going to be hard on you unless you get out of line, but if you do, I can tell you, I'm no easy guy to deal with." His chin came forward again, and his hands came back to his hips. "I'm not saying that I'll use force on you. But I have some rules, and—"

"So what kind of offense are we going to use?"

"Listen, uh, Noodle. I'm going to get to that. First I want to set down the rules."

"Dad, we don't need any rules. We never had any before."

Mr. Nutsell gave a knowing nod, allowed himself just a little smile. "And you never *won* before, son. That's why some things are going to change around here."

But Noodle wasn't giving up. "Last year we tried to use that weave thing for an offense, and we kept bumping into each other. It was like an eggbeater. Do you have some good plays we can use?"

"Well . . . sure. We'll have some plays."

"Like what?"

"We'll get to that later."

Orlando leaned over to Nutty. "He doesn't know any plays, does he?"

"No. I told you that. But we had to have a coach or they wouldn't let us play in the league."

Noodle wasn't finished yet. "Are we going to use a high post or a low post or what?"

"Well . . . we'll probably use both at different times. A good team has to take advantage of the other team's weaknesses, you know. We'll put the shortest guys at guard, the tallest at center, and the in-between ones at forward. And then we'll have the guards bring the ball down the court, and we'll use the center for the post."

"The man is a genius," Orlando whispered.

"Shut up," Nutty said, but he was embarrassed. All the guys were looking around at each other. Nutty knew they were thinking the same thing as Orlando. Nutty had to do something. "Dad," he said, "why don't we get started practicing, instead of just talking so much?"

"Well, I wanted to establish a few things first. We need to . . ."

But all the guys had liked Nutty's idea; they were heading out of the bleachers, grabbing the balls and running for the baskets. Mr. Nutsell tried his whistle, but no one seemed to notice.

Orlando was right behind Nutty. "This isn't going to work," he said. "Nothing against your dad, but he doesn't know what he's doing."

"Right. Nothing against him." Nutty felt like punching Orlando—but he knew he was right.

Richie and Bilbo were coming over now. Bilbo was shaking his head. "Nutty, nothing against your dad, but—"

"Look, I've had enough of this 'nothing against your dad' stuff. I never said he knew a lot about basketball. I just said maybe he would do it. We had to find someone."

"Yeah, but you didn't warn us about all the rah-rah stuff," Richie said. "Is he going to keep doing that?"

Nutty couldn't look anyone in the eye. "Probably. He's always like that. You ought to know him that well by now."

"Well, we've got to do something," Orlando said. "We don't need a cheerleader. We need someone who knows some plays."

Mr. Nutsell was blowing his whistle again. "All right, fellows, let's get started."

"Are we going to do some drills?" Noodle was asking.

"Well, yes. We'll do drills. But a good team is built on a good attitude, and I want to talk to you about attitude before we actually start working out."

"Nutty," Bilbo said, "we're in trouble."

Nutty was thinking. But as always, when he got in a real bind, the first thing that came to mind was that he'd better get help from a mind better than his own. "I think I'll have a talk with William tonight," he said.

"William Bilks? What can he do? He's never played basketball in his life."

That was true, and Nutty had no idea what he could do, but William had never let the boys down before. If nothing else, his opinion was worth having.

"Now, listen," Mr. Nutsell was saying. "I want you to think about the whole purpose of athletic competition. It's all a game, of course, and yet it's not a game at all. It's life, even though it isn't life. It's the chance to go out there and discover who you are, what you're made of, and to do it where it doesn't matter—except, of course, that it really does matter. All the pain and joy of life can be felt on the athletic field, and so in a way it is life, and what that means is that in a game setting you find out whether you're up to the challenge to face life when it actually is life—real life."

"I think I got lost somewhere in there," Orlando said.

"The next thing you know," Bilbo whispered, "he'll be talking about the thrill of victory and the agony of defeat."

"When you win, you'll know what the term 'the thrill of victory' means, and when . . ."

"Oh, brother," Nutty moaned.

CHAPTER TWO

Nutty rode home with his dad from practice. Or maybe "practice" wasn't the right word. They never did play a whole lot of basketball. Dad had given a very long, very punchy talk about attitude. Nutty had never heard his dad get quite so carried away. He had told stories about great athletes, war heroes, presidents, business leaders, and great insurance salesmen, sometimes hinting at himself as an example.

"You know, Freddie," he said, as he drove along, "I think I really got to the guys. At first they merely wanted to get back out on the court and shoot the ball around, but I noticed that as they listened, they started to catch the vision. I saw that far-off look in their eyes. I think they were trying to look beyond the present and see their own futures."

They were falling asleep, Nutty thought, but he didn't say it.

"A game like basketball is mostly mental, you know. It's drive. It's believing in yourself. It's that extra push when the sweat is running down your face and you're running out of breath. I'll tell you what it is: It's the American spirit. That's why America plays this game better than anyone. We've got the kind of spirit it takes to play a game like basketball. And I'll tell you what else: There's not a better way in the world to find out who you really are, to put yourself on the line and—"

"I know, Dad. You mentioned that. But we need some plays too."

Mr. Nutsell appeared to squirm a little. He glanced over at Nutty. "Did you actually have plays last year, or did you—"

"Yeah, we had plays. We just couldn't make them work. Mr. Stinski had us all weave around the post, but we were always running in circles, getting all mixed up, and the other team would just wait until we threw the ball away or traveled or something. We were terrible."

"Now, see, that's just the thing. You can make this game too complicated. That's the last thing I want to do. I think you come down the floor—with a lot of confidence and a great attitude—and you pass the ball around until you get an open shot, and then you take it and make it. There's something to say for simplicity."

"Yeah, but you've gotta get open, Dad. That's what the plays help you do. And our guys don't shoot too well. If we can get some shots from close in we've got a lot better chance."

"Maybe we should just practice shooting a lot."

"Dad, we still need plays."

"Oh, sure. Sure. I know that."

"Do you know any?"

"Well, I . . . have some ideas. What sort of plays do the other teams use?"

"I'm not sure. I hear them talking about screens and give-and-go plays, and stuff like that."

"And what, exactly, do they mean by that, Freddie?"

Oh, brother. The Lab School Labradors were in real trouble. Nutty didn't push the matter any further. He thought for a moment of picking up a book on basketball at the library, something to learn some strategy from, but he knew what Dad would say: "You can't learn to play basketball from a book, for crying out loud." Nutty knew he'd better get over to William's house as quickly as he could.

As soon as Nutty got home he called William, who checked his appointment book and then agreed to have Nutty come at seven-fifteen. At dinner Nutty asked his parents whether it was all right to go. He told them that he needed some help from William with his math, which was true, if not quite the whole story.

It was very cold out, and as Nutty walked to William's house, all bundled up, he kept thinking that a lot of the school year had already gone by. It was January, and the year was almost half over. His term as Student Council president would be over before he knew it, and he wasn't really sure he had accomplished much. The ski trip he had organized at Christmastime had been great (except for a few problems) but not all that many of the kids had been able to go. What the school really needed was something to give it a little pride. The sports teams were usually pretty bad. There simply weren't enough kids to choose from. If just once they could have a great team, that would really help.

William seemed glad to see Nutty, although he showed it in typical William Bilks formal style. "Hello, Nutty. Nice of you to come over. I've not heard much from you since our ski adventure." He sounded like Nutty's grandpa, but he looked like one of Santa's plump little elves. He had on a sweater with the front all buttoned up, and his hair was combed very nicely, as though he had spruced up a little for his "guest."

"It's been too cold to go anywhere," Nutty said.

"Yes, yes. That's quite true. Now tell me, what is this business about basketball you wanted to discuss? I've always been quite a baseball fan, and I enjoy track events, but I've never paid as much attention to basketball."

"Yeah, I know. But we need help . . . bad."

William had Nutty sit down on a chair near the foot of his bed, and then he sat down in the chair at his desk and swiveled around. His feet barely reached the floor to do the swiveling.

"Whatever could *I* do?"

"Well, I'm not sure. I've been thinking about that. The thing is, my dad is supposed to be coaching us."

"Oh, dear."

"What's that supposed to mean?" Nutty was getting a little defensive about what appeared to be a more and more common attitude toward his father.

"Excuse me. I was only thinking that a coach must be careful to take a practical approach. I'm afraid your father might tend to get rather wrapped up in his own language. The man does get carried away."

Nutty knew that William had a point. "That's just the thing, William. He agreed to coach, but he doesn't really know the game very well. He doesn't know anything about offense or defense or anything."

"Maybe he understands the rest of the game," William said, and chuckled to himself. But then he added, in a more serious tone, "Are you thinking that I could somehow invent some plays for you?"

"I guess so. Maybe I could just slip them to Dad and— No, wait a minute. What if you were our assistant coach? You could—"

"Nutty, please. That's hardly feasible. After all, I'm eleven years old, the same as you."

"How many eleven-year-olds take college classes in the evenings after spending all day at a private school?"

"Very few, of course. But a coach needs a certain amount of presence, a way with young men. I think in many ways it's a matter of charisma and leadership. I really doubt I could manage all that, although I do have a certain force of personality, when I assert myself."

"Look, Dad could worry about the leadership and all that other stuff. He can give the big speeches. You would come up with practice drills and offensive and defensive plans. I know you could do it."

"But Nutty, I already told you: I know little about the game."

"Get some books. Read up on it, and then watch some games on TV. I'll bet—with your mind—you could be picking apart defenses in no time. You'd know just what to do. We all know you're a genius."

"Well, admittedly, my analytical skills would help, and I'm good at the sort of research you're suggesting. But I'm not sure that I have the time or interest for such a big undertaking." He was drumming his fingers against his rounded stomach, leaning back. Despite what William was saying, Nutty could see "that look." William loved a challenge, and his life sometimes lacked variety.

If it weren't for Nutty he might never do anything but study.

Nutty decided to go for the sale. He knew how William's mind worked. "William, a lot of guys need you. We've won only one game in two years—and that was because a team didn't show up on time and had to forfeit. But more than that, the whole lab school needs a lift. We do great on achievement tests and stuff like that, but we never *win* anything. Kids at other schools think we're just a bunch of brains who can only do well in school, but we're more than that. We need to show people that kids with minds can also compete with their bodies."

"This all surprises me," William said, hardly showing the reaction Nutty had hoped for.

"Surprises you? Why?"

"I had no idea that the students at the lab school were considered superior in intelligence. Do people actually include people like you and Orlando in this stereotype you speak of?"

"Well, sure. I'm a good student."

"Really? Then why do you come to me for help on your math?"

"William, I'm a good student. You're a computer. Lots of good students use computers."

William chuckled. "Really, I'm hardly a—"

"Will you do it? If nothing else, prove that *you* can compete in athletics. Show people that brains are better than muscle when it comes to sports."

"Well, it is a combination, of course. But you do have a point."

"Will you do it, then?"

"Let me think about it. I'll check the university library tomorrow and see what books on basketball strategy are available, and I'll have a hard look at my time. Why don't you give me your practice and playing schedule, so that I can see how it would fit with my own priorities?"

Nutty explained the schedule, and answered William's other questions, and the next morning he told Bilbo and Orlando that he thought he had an assistant coach who could solve all their problems.

"Coach? William?" Orlando said. "You've gotta be kidding. The other team would laugh us off the court. How can we show up at games with an eleven-year-old coach?"

"Look, William is only eleven in the sense that—"

"I know that. I know how smart he is. But that doesn't make him a basketball coach. What does he know about basketball?"

"He's going to study up on it. He'll figure out some great plays, and he'll be able to look at defenses and know exactly what to do."

"Nutty, you're nuts. You can't learn basketball from a book."

"He learned to ski from a book, and he skied better than you did."

"No way. He just had a knack for skiing; that book didn't help him."

Nutty looked at Bilbo. Bilbo was a reader. Maybe he would have a little more respect for what a brain could do to compete with muscle and height and strength, and all the other things the Lab School Labradors had very little of.

"It'll never work," Bilbo said.

"Thanks a million," Nutty said. "But look, it's worth a shot. If my dad tries to coach us without any help, we know we're in trouble."

For that one, the boys had no answer.

CHAPTER THREE

William agreed to be the assistant coach. He called that night and told Nutty that he had done some reading about basketball strategy and actually found himself "quite intrigued. It's much like chess in many ways. I feel confident that we can win."

Nutty liked the sound of that. What he didn't like was the idea of breaking the news to his dad; so he simply told William to show up for the next practice. And then, in front of all the players, he announced that William was willing to help out with coaching the team. Dad looked shocked, but Nutty whispered, "Dad, he can't really play. Helping out with coaching will be a way for him to get involved in sports a little. I think he needs something like that."

It worked, of course. "Well, that's a good point, Freddie," his dad said. "I can probably use him. I'll have him help with some of the drills."

That's how it started. Ten minutes later, William was asking Mr. Nutsell whether he would mind stepping back, because he was getting in the boys' way. William began to introduce agility drills that he had learned from the books he had read.

Nutty took the chance to move in close to his dad. "He really knows his drills, doesn't he? I told him that if he wanted to help, he could read up a little. Everything he knows he got from a book, though. He doesn't have any experience. I hope you don't mind."

"Well, no. I don't mind. Assistant coaches usually help quite a lot with drills. I just . . . well, I think he's a little pushy, if you want to know the truth."

Nutty had noticed that some of the guys were not too thrilled either when William started to tell them what to do, but once they got into the drills, and saw how they worked, they seemed not to care whose ideas they were.

"Yeah, I know, Dad. That's a problem of William's. You'll just have to make sure he knows who the boss is."

"Don't worry about that." Mr. Nutsell threw his shoulders back, and then he brought his whistle to his lips and blew it. "All right," he yelled. "That's excellent. We appreciate our assistant's teaching those agility drills. In fact, I think I'll have him in charge of our opening drills every day. That will be very helpful to me. But now, fellows, why don't you get down on one knee here for just a moment."

"Oh, brother. Here we go," Orlando whispered to Nutty.

"I like what I just saw out there," Mr. Nutsell was saying. "I saw a lot of aggressiveness, a lot of confidence. I saw young men who have said to themselves, 'We're winners.' And the reason you are winners is that deep within yourselves you know who you are. And what you know is that—"

"Mr. Nutsell, are we going to get some plays today?" Some of the guys started to laugh, but Noodle seemed concerned.

"Noodle—John, that is—I wish you wouldn't do that. We'll start working on plays when I tell you it's time. Right now I think we need to work on basics: dribbling, passing, shooting. And above all, we need to get ourselves into a winning frame of mind. So much of winning is the way you think about what you're doing. That's why I'm emphasizing the importance of—"

"What about defense? Are we going to play man-to-man or zone or what?"

Orlando was losing it. He was trying hard not to laugh, but little snickers were sneaking out. "Shut up," Nutty whispered, but he himself was struggling not to laugh.

"I haven't decided yet about the defense. We'll be scrimmaging one of these days, and we'll have to do some experimenting."

"How can we scrimmage if we don't know any plays? And besides that, we only have eight guys."

"Noodle, you let me do the coaching around here, all right? If you're not satisfied with the job I'm doing, find yourself a better coach."

"My dad works evenings."

Mr. Nutsell was shifting from one foot to the other, looking more than a little upset. His voice was tight as a violin string. Everyone could see he was about to lose his temper—everyone except Noodle, anyway. Noodle was sitting Indian style, his long legs wound like a pretzel, and his face looked as innocent as a baby's—or maybe it just looked sort of blank.

"Mr. Nutsell." It was William. "I was just thinking. It might not hurt to learn a couple of basic offensive plays. They could practice dribbling and passing and shooting as they executed them. I have a couple in mind that might work very well. They're simple but, I think, quite effective."

Mr. Nutsell cleared his throat. He fidgeted a little, playing with his whistle, but he was nodding and looking quite thoughtful. "Well now, William, that may not be a bad idea. I've said all along that I think simplicity is the essence of a game like this, at least for young people. If you know a couple of good, simple plays, it might be well to teach those to the boys. I'm not a man who is too proud to let you young people lead. I happen to believe that the young people of today are some of the most remarkable individuals ever to—"

"Should I just go ahead then?"

"Well, yes. You show them the basic patterns, and I'll take over from there."

"I have some designs for zone defenses too, and some good basic tips for man-to-man defense."

"That's fine, William. Just fine. I'm perfectly willing to accept your input. I don't feel that just because I'm older than you are, there's anything superior about the plays I might use."

William took over. Mr. Nutsell occasionally gave some advice, usually associated with a positive attitude, but William ran the rest of the practice. He taught the boys what he called the "basic cut movement" offense. He lined up Noodle at high post and taught the guys how to cut off the center, and then he showed them the various pass options. By the end of the next practice, they were looking pretty fair; by the end of the week they were really starting to believe in themselves.

Mr. Nutsell was catching on to the drills and the plays himself. He sometimes sounded a bit like an echo machine, simply repeating the things William was saying. He showed them some plays himself, however, and the boys' attitudes were getting better all the time. He finished each practice with a powerful speech—although most of the boys said they had to leave and didn't stay for the whole thing. Nutty was the only one who always stayed to the bitter end. He also heard additional speeches on the way home, at home, at dinner, breakfast, and during in-between-meal snacks.

Nutty's mom seemed to think it was all rather funny. She told him this coaching job was wonderful for Dad and she was glad the two of them were enjoying something together. Nutty felt sort of guilty about the things he had thought, even said, about his dad's lectures, and he tried to convince himself that maybe some of those talks were doing some good, since the guys really did seem to be improving.

And then the first game came along. It was against the Ridge View Raiders. These guys had won the championship every season for years. They were big, and they were good, and they knew it.

But that didn't worry the lab school Labradors. They were confident. Maybe they were still wearing those ugly brown uniforms the team had owned for years (brown had been on sale, and "Gee, boys, some Labradors are brown, aren't they?"), but the guys went out on the floor and ran their plays. The only problem was, the Raiders' defense kept getting in the way. It was really frustrating. When the Labradors tried to pass the ball, some kid in a red uniform would be there. When they tried to dribble, someone would knock the ball out of their hands. And when they tried to take a shot, defenders would guard them so closely that they were lucky to get the shot off, let alone score.

William called a time out; or that is to say, Mr. Nutsell called it, after William suggested the idea. The score was already 8 to 0. All the guys walked over to the side, looking bewildered. "What's going on?" Noodle was saying. "Those guys won't let us do our plays."

Mr. Nutsell stepped forward, but all the guys walked past him to William. "Why aren't you guys doing what I taught you?" William asked. He looked as baffled as the rest.

"They keep getting in our way," Noodle said.

"William," Nutty said, "they have a good defense. They're big and quick, and they're playing a really tight man-to-man."

"Yes, but in the diagrams, when you cut off the post, the defender is supposed to get screened out, and you're supposed to get an open shot."

"Geez, William," Orlando said, "I told you it wasn't as easy as you thought. It doesn't work just the way you draw it on a diagram."

"Why not?"

"Oh, brother. Nutty, tell him."

"Well, William, they're fast. They may get screened, but they recover and get back to us just when we're trying to shoot. It's not as easy as you think."

"No, I guess not."

"So what do we do?"

William just stared. Nutty could see that he had no idea. But Mr. Nutsell had an answer. He used William's confusion to assert himself. "All right, boys, now listen to me. I think all this cutting stuff is only getting you messed up. I want you to come down the floor, pass the ball around, hit the open man, and pop that old ball through the hoop. I know you can do it. There's not a doubt in my mind, and there should be none in yours. We've got these guys right where we want them. They're so overconfident, they think all they have to do is walk out there and they'll win. They remind me of—"

The referee was telling the boys to move onto the floor. Orlando walked back with Nutty. "We couldn't beat these guys if we had to. They're better than we are."

"Where's your positive attitude?" Nutty asked.

"I think that big guy in the red shirt took it away from me. He's got two of them now."

Nutty was too miserable to laugh. He looked over at the Raiders' bench, where the other team was doing enough laughing without his help. He was just glad the gym was almost empty. At least not too many spectators were there to see the massacre.

Things only got worse. The Labradors gave up on the cutting offense, but now it was a free-for-all. They tried to pass the ball around; but the guys from Ridge View were too quick, and they kept making steals. Orlando kept trying to show off his great dribbling ability, but when he did, the defense seemed to know that it was just a matter of time before he kicked the ball out-of-bounds, double dribbled, or forgot where he was on the floor.

Noodle was tall enough to get a couple of rebounds and he managed to score. But he was so skinny that when he went inside, he got pounded. It wasn't long until he was hanging back. Nutty scored a couple of baskets—but he shot about twenty times, usually from way out, which was about the only place where he could get a clear shot.

It was a nightmare. Ridge View had one gigantic player named Erin something or other. He scored almost any time he wanted to. By the last quarter only Ridge View's subs were playing, and the guys on the bench were spending all their time laughing. "Hey, number twelve," they kept yelling—twelve was Nutty—"try another shot from half court. Last time you *almost* hit the rim."

Noodle took so much ribbing (for one thing about his ribs) that he came very close to breaking down and crying. William—or Mr. Nutsell—took him out of the game and let some of the other guys play. Mirkle was a disaster, and Pandelli was worse. But having those two on the floor at the same time with Gary Goutz gave a whole new meaning to the word *embarrassment*. What they were doing looked more like bumper cars than basketball. The Raiders were laughing so hard they could hardly play.

It really didn't matter much anyway. The game was out of hand. The agony of defeat was one thing; slow death by torture was a little hard to take.

Orlando finally lost his cool and tried to punch one of the Ridge View players, but the kid put his hand on little Orlando's chest, held him away, and said, "I would like to hurt you, kid. It would be fun. But I feel too sorry for you."

That sort of summed up the game. Or maybe 69 to 13 summed it up pretty well too.

CHAPTER FOUR

Nutty decided to walk home from the game with William. It was not even noon yet, and Nutty didn't want to get home too fast. It could be a long day. He knew his dad would have plenty to say.

The weather was not quite so cold as it had been, and Nutty enjoyed the cool air. He blew his breath out as he walked, watched the steam float away. "Boy, did we stink," he said. "We're no better than we were last year."

"Yes, you really were quite awful," William said. "I had no idea."

"Thanks."

"Those other fellows were so much bigger, and they were much more proficient in ball handling and shooting."

"Look, William, if you want to quit coaching, that's okay. We'll just do what we do every year—lose all our games. Dad can handle that kind of coaching as well as you can."

"Yes, I suppose." But William was thinking. Nutty could almost hear the computer whirring in William's head. That was a good sign—the most hopeful that Nutty had seen since the game started.

They walked more than a block before William said anything. Missouri had gotten more snow than usual so far this winter, and Warrensburg had been hit especially hard right after Christmas. The snow was piled up on both sides of the sidewalk, but at least, with the warmer weather, the walks were mostly clear.

"My mistakes came from inexperience," William said.

"*Your* mistakes? We're the ones who couldn't make the plays work."

"Yes, of course. But I should have foreseen that. On paper it was all a chess game, and I could see exactly how it would work. I hadn't accounted for differences in skill and quickness—and size."

"There's not that much you can do when the other team is ten times better than your own. If they were only a little better, we could maybe match them with good plays, but those guys were . . ."

"Yes, they were. But I'm not sure that certain adjustments couldn't be made."

"William, we need a whole lot more than adjustments."

William was thinking again. It was hard for Nutty to imagine that the Labradors would ever have any hope against the Ridge View team, but maybe some of the other teams in the league weren't very good. And one thing about William—if there was a way, he would find it.

"Have you ever heard of imaging?" William finally said.

"Imagining?"

"No. Imaging. It's a new technique being used by some athletes. It's a matter of picturing yourself doing things well, envisioning yourself being successful. Athletes who see themselves winning or at least doing well seem to perform at higher levels. I read a little about it the other day when I was browsing in the library."

"Sounds like my dad's positive-thinking stuff."

"Well, no. It's not psyching yourself up, or telling yourself how good you are. It's actually *seeing* yourself in the act of doing what you want to do. It's a form of mental preparation."

"William, we need a whole lot more than mental preparation. We need to learn how to dribble and shoot."

"Yes, that's just the point."

"What's the point?"

"Well, think about it this way. Supposing a computerized robot were to be taught basketball. If it were sophisticated enough, it could calculate the distance to the hoop, the required trajectory, and the necessary force, and it could loft the ball to the basket perfectly. Wouldn't you agree?"

"Sure. Maybe we could recruit one for our team. That's what we need."

"But we already have a number of them—a whole team of them."

"William, excuse me, but you've lost me." The boys had stopped at a signal light. Nutty turned and looked down at William. "If you think Orlando is a basketball robot, you weren't watching very closely today."

"Well, let's think about it. Orlando—or any of you—has all the needed mechanisms. You have eyes that can zero in on the basket. You have a brain that is more sophisticated than any computer. It can calculate distance and trajectory. Your arm and hand are a magnificent piece of machinery, much more refined than any robot arm. I suspect that if the mind and arm were left to operate without interference, the two of them could loft a perfect shot every single time."

Nutty had to think about that. He knew it couldn't be that simple, but he wasn't sure why. At last he said, "William, no offense, but I think you're looking at this like chess again. The pros, the greatest players who ever played the game, practice all the time and play a zillion games. They're considered great shooters if they can sink their shots a little better than half the time."

"Yes, of course. I'm not entirely ignorant about the game. But the question is, why do they sometimes miss? I suspect that the mind and arm get out of sync because of various disturbances: crowd noise, distracting thoughts, doubts, all sorts of things."

"Well, if those guys can't get that stuff out of their heads, who can?"

"I don't know. Maybe you can."

"William, that's impossible. I'm not a good shooter to start with."

But William was paying no attention; he was thinking again. Nutty was getting cold, and now that he could see what William had in mind, he was losing any hope that something could be done to improve the team. William was really barking up the wrong tree this time. Orlando a robot? That wasn't the wrong tree—that was the wrong forest.

"Nutty, do you know how to type?"

"No."

"Too bad. You'll have to trust me on this. Once a person has learned the touch method of typing, he or she can sit down at a typewriter or computer, look at words on a page, and automatically, without thinking about it, reproduce those words perfectly. No thought is necessary. The fingers know exactly what to do. In fact—and here is the crucial point—the fingers do a better job if the typist does *not* think about the act of typing. The eye sees the letters, and the brain, unconsciously, processes the image and sends the corresponding signals to the fingers."

"So you're saying a guy should just shoot and not think?"

"Yes. But more than that, shooting should become automatic, a function of the unconscious mind, with no cognitive processing."

"Come on, William, I don't know what you're talking about now."

"Okay, let me explain it this way. Have you ever seen a basketball player get what they call 'hot'?"

"Sure. Some nights a guy just can't miss."

"Why?"

"I don't know. He just . . . gets hot."

"Don't you see? The mechanism *has* to be mental. The arm and body don't change. But players will even say, 'The guy was unconscious; he couldn't miss.' I've watched the sports news on television and heard them say those very words. And the guy who can't miss will tell you that he knew the ball was going in when it left his hand. Somehow the process becomes automatic, like typing."

"So how come no one can do it all the time?"

"I'm not sure. I suspect that players practice the physical moves, such as shooting—which is necessary—but they don't practice enough with their minds. I also suspect that the state of being 'hot' could be pushed to perfection if a player could get beyond all the conscious confusion and enter a mental state something like a hypnotic trance."

"You're going to try to hypnotize us, aren't you? I can see it coming."

"Not exactly. And certainly not the whole team. Actually, I'm not sure what I'm going to do. First I'm going to do some more thinking and reading. Will you at least agree to try some experimenting, Nutty?"

"Why me? Let's try all the guys. We all need it."

"Well, until I know more what I'm doing, that might be counterproductive. For now, let's see what we can do with you. Let's start on Monday. I can't commit more than an hour a day, but I'll give that much, if you will."

They had reached William's house and stopped out in front. "That's okay with me," Nutty said. "But I don't think it will work."

"Perhaps not. But at least in my system you won't be required to think positively. You'll be required to think not at all, and over the last year I've found that you do have some talent in that area."

Nutty had thanked William and walked several steps away before he realized he had been insulted. But he really didn't care. He had been on the receiving end of enough cheap shots already that day—one more from William hardly mattered.

When Nutty got home his dad was fixing himself a huge sandwich for lunch. "Want one?" he asked. He sounded depressed.

"No, thanks."

"I think a lot of the problem was with those plays William wanted you to do," Dad said.

At that point, Mom came through the door from the garage. "What was? Did those guys beat you?"

"*Beat* is too nice a word for what they did, Mom. *Battered, abused, assaulted, trampled.* Words like that might come a little closer."

"William taught them a complicated bunch of plays, and they just didn't work. That got them discouraged. And once they lost their confidence, it was all over."

"Dad, it wouldn't have mattered. The Raiders are so much better than we are that—"

"There it goes. The whole season. You keep talking like that and we might as well turn out the lights and sing 'The Party's Over.'"

Mom put her arm around Nutty's shoulders. Her furry coat was cold, even through his shirt. "The only thing that really matters is that you had fun. Did you have fun, honey?"

"No. I had no fun at all."

Dad, in the background, was saying, "Oh, for heaven's sake. Don't start pumping that kind of hogwash into him. He'll be a loser for sure."

And Susie, Nutty's little sister, who had just entered the scene, offered her opinion that Nutty was a klutz and so were all his friends.

Mrs. Nutsell somehow found all this amusing, and began to laugh, but Nutty didn't. And so he escaped to his bedroom. He had been there only a couple of minutes, however, when his mother called him to the phone. He expected that Orlando or Bilbo might be calling, so he was surprised to hear a girl's voice.

"Nutty, this is Sarah. I was wondering how the game turned out."

Sarah Montag. Nutty had known her since they were both just little kids. But lately he had started to . . . notice her. He wasn't sure whether she had gotten pretty, or whether she always had been and he hadn't paid any attention. Of course, he would never tell anyone in the world that he thought about such things.

"We got mutilated."

"Oh, really? I'm supposed to write a story about it for the school paper, but I couldn't get there. The game was right at the same time as my gymnastics class."

"Don't put it in the paper. Just pretend it didn't happen."

"The way you guys were talking this week, I thought you were going to have a good team this year."

"Yeah, well, that's what it was: talk. We won't be bragging next week."

"Well . . . I'm sorry."

"That's okay."

"You don't even want to tell me the score?"

"Especially not the score."

She waited for a time, and then she said, "But I'll bet *you* played well, didn't you?"

There was something in her voice. Something that made a tingle go up his neck. When he went back to his room, he couldn't stop thinking about it. He wished he had been good. In fact, all of a sudden, he wished that he had been fantastic. Amazing. The greatest player ever.

Something strange was going on. Nutty had never felt this way before.

CHAPTER FIVE

Nutty devoted a lot of the next week to basketball, even though he had little hope for better results. On Monday William suggested that Nutty begin his new program by staying after school every day and practicing his shooting.

Some of the other guys did that too, although they spent more time goofing off than practicing. Orlando kept getting Richie into games of H-O-R-S-E, trying all kinds of impossible shots that he would never try in a game. Bilbo usually didn't last long. He preferred to go home and read. Noodle and a few of the other guys joined them a couple of times, and they too seemed to lack interest in working very hard.

On Tuesday and Thursday Mr. Nutsell directed the practice. He had decided to take back the reins of leadership from William, and he gave quite a strong speech about the mistakes they had made the week before, implying that William had been a big part of the problem. "We don't need a complicated offense. We need a group of young men ready to give their all. Now you're going to find out who you are. You can either give up and be losers, or you can pull yourselves up by the bootstraps and go after this next team. The whole reason to play the game is to discover what is inside you."

Orlando was leaning back, staring at the ceiling. "I know what's inside me," he whispered. "Intestines, liver, gall bladder—it's a real mess in there."

William, for some reason, seemed willing to accept all the blame. Mr. Nutsell told the boys to forget about all their plays and just practice passing the ball around and taking any good shots they happened to see. It was mass confusion, but that didn't seem to concern anyone.

But William did not just sit idly by. He talked to Nutty, mainly about getting himself open for shots on the "perimeter." "I noticed last week that if you want to take quite a long shot, guys usually won't guard you too close."

"Sure they won't," Nutty said. "That's because no one can hit anything from that far out."

"You will, once we get going with your imaging," William said, but Nutty gave no proof whatsoever that such a thing was going to happen. His shooting was improving some, which meant that he often came close, even with his long shots, but he still rarely sank the ball.

Dad usually gave him a chewing out for shooting from so far away. "Work it in, Freddie," he would yell. And of course they could do that when they were practicing against their own guys, all three of them. Nutty knew it would be another story against teams like Ridge View and Reese.

After working with the team in the gym came the real workout. William came over every evening, and they sat in Nutty's room and worked on "imaging."

William would talk Nutty through the mental practice. "The ball leaves your hand, with a perfect snap of the wrist, leaves your fingertips with perfect back spin and arches perfectly through the air. It does not touch the rim. It snaps into the net and drops through with a swish. But you feel no joy in that. You do not think about it. You cannot miss, and you cannot feel. You are a shooting machine."

Nutty would lie on his bed and concentrate. In his mind he would see the ball arch through the air and swish through the basket—a perfect shot every time. The truth was, however, that it wasn't so easy as it might seem. His imagination sometimes took over from his image making, and it would throw in a little variety: air balls, shots that spun around the rim and didn't go down, even one shot that stopped halfway there and came back. But Nutty never admitted such things to William. He wasn't taking the whole idea very seriously, if the truth were known, despite William's dedication.

Actually Nutty quite enjoyed the image when he could see it in his mind and didn't let something else happen. The only thing that started to make him feel like a machine was going over and over the same shots so many times.

About midweek William introduced something new. He brought a little gold basketball on a chain. He swung it in front of Nutty's eyes, telling him that all else was gone, that only Nutty and his arm and the basketball existed. The ball was an extension of his mind and arm, and these three elements understood each other entirely. He told Nutty to shut his eyes and see the mental ball passing from his mind and arm into the net.

Nutty saw it all, and he did pass into some sort of hypnotic state—either that or he was so tired he was dozing off. In any case, he was getting better at watching the ball in his head go into the basket; the only trouble was, the ball he played with at the gym was not cooperating much better than it ever had.

That Friday, William decided it was time to bring mind and reality together. William came over to the school and, once all the other guys had given up and gone home, told Nutty it was time to show that he could do it.

Nutty had been shooting the ball, trying to use his concentration; but it was hard to do with his eyes open, and shutting them didn't work, either. He walked over to the bleachers, where William was sitting. "William, I hate to tell you, but all that imaging stuff hasn't helped me at all. I'm shooting a little better, but I think that's just because I've been practicing a lot this week."

"We haven't really begun the meshing of the physical and mental. That's what we're going to do now. Sit down." He got out his little gold basketball.

"Geez, William, what if someone walks in here. They'll think we're nuts, you swinging that little thing around and me staring at it."

"No one ever understands great innovators, Nutty. We can't worry about that. Besides, I locked the door."

"Well, good." Nutty got himself comfortable, leaning back, but he couldn't help smiling.

"What now?"

"This is crazy, William. I've always thought you were pretty down-to-earth, but you'll have to admit this is kind of wild."

"I admit nothing of the sort. It's scientifically sound. And it's the very doubts you have that cause it not to work. That's why others have failed to cross the boundaries into ultimate trust. Your mind and body know exactly what to do; it's your conscious confusion that interferes. Now, give up all that. Relax and let yourself enter a state of complete 'otherness.'"

"Sure thing." But he was still smiling.

It took several minutes to get Nutty into his trance. He wasn't asleep or anything like that. In fact, he had the feeling he was just taking it easy. All the same, something strange was happening to him again. It was as though the basketball, first the gold one and then the one in his mind, turned into the whole world—it was all he could see, and it was empowered to do his will. He watched it loop into the basket time and time again, with never a miss. He no longer had trouble seeing it, and it never failed to do what he commanded.

When William told him to get up and open his eyes, Nutty felt strange: the way he had felt lately when they had practiced at home. The gym—everything outside himself—seemed more distant than usual. It was all there, but not clearly visible, as though it were hovering just beyond his consciousness.

"All right, Nutty. Now go out on the court and look at the basket. Concentrate on the hoop."

Nutty felt light; he was walking on the floor but felt nothing beneath his feet. His eyes did not move from the basket. When he reached the top of the key, he began to envision himself shooting.

"Now try a couple of shots without the ball. Just let your body do what it's supposed to do."

Nutty dribbled the nonexistent ball to his right, and then he pulled up and took a jump shot. He watched the ball snap into the net. William handed him another, and once again he took a jump shot and saw the imaginary ball hit the net without touching the rim. He sank a few more that way, and he found himself believing he really was shooting something.

And then, the next time, the ball he held was real—he felt the texture. But it wasn't that much of a change. He dribbled to his right again, lifted the ball to his chest and then he leaped—just sort of sailed, really—into the air. His arm cocked and the ball came up. Then his arm pushed forward; his wrist snapped, and the ball spun off his hands. A perfect arch, and then—*swish.*

"Oh, my gosh, it worked," Nutty said. He spun around and looked at William. "I did it. It worked. I can't believe it."

"Calm down. Don't say that. Don't let your conscious mind take over. Just do it again." William waddled off after the ball. He picked it up and gave it an awkward two-hand shove back toward Nutty.

"This is going to work," Nutty said. "It's fantastic." He dribbled again and took the same jump shot—and missed net, hoop, backboard, everything.

"That's what I was afraid of," William said. "You let yourself get too satisfied with yourself, and you started to think of what you were doing. You have to get back to that automatic state you were in for a minute or so."

"But I'll always get excited when I make a shot. You can't expect me not to feel anything."

"Yes I can. That's exactly why no one has ever mastered the technique. The great players get hot, can't miss, and then they start to think too much. They get cocky, or they get scared they'll start missing, or scared they'll lose, or glad they're winning—whatever. But when the thoughts start, the mind gets out of sync again, and it all goes down the drain."

"So I've got to shoot and not feel anything? Not even think about it?"

"Exactly."

"Oh, wow. I don't think I can do that."

"Yes you can. Don't say you can't." And the two went back to the bleachers and started over. William swung the gold basketball, talked Nutty deep into his trance, and then came back to the floor for some imaginary shooting. Then the ball was there again. And Nutty snapped off a shot that swished the net. Another shot, another swish.

Somewhere from deep inside, Nutty was watching all this, and he felt comfortable, as though he were in a pleasant dream, knew he was dreaming, but didn't mind. The ball kept snapping from his fingers, swishing, swishing, arching perfectly, swishing, over and over. Somewhere out there was a regular world. But to Nutty the world was nothing but a hoop, a ball, and the touch of the ball in his hands, rolling from his fingers as his wrist snapped.

And then there was a yell. "Twenty. That's *twenty*, Nutty! You just hit twenty in a row."

"What?"

"Oh, I'm sorry. I shouldn't have gotten so excited."

"I hit twenty shots in a row from clear out *here*?"

"Yes. You did it."

"Why did you stop me?"

"I'm sorry. But you're going to have to get used to people cheering and yelling. That will be the tough test. Maybe that's why even the pros can't do it."

Nutty looked up at the hoop. "I think I can do it," he said, softly. "I sort of like what happens. It's just me and the ball."

"Yes, yes. You've got it, Nutty. Tomorrow you don't have to miss—not at all. We'll get you ready for the game, and you won't miss, Nutty. You *can't* miss."

Nutty almost believed it. He went home that night and spent most of the evening in his room. He lay on his bed and watched the ball travel to the hoop, as though his eyes could guide it like a missile under his control. He saw it pass through the basket, and something like electricity seemed to move through the air, giving him a gentle rush of satisfaction. It wasn't elation, just gentle pleasure, but he liked it.

Nutty liked to picture it all: the ball leaving his hand, floating quietly, hitting nothing but net. The crowd was out there somewhere, but that didn't mean much; what he liked best was the simple, calm confidence he felt—something he had never known in his life.

And then Sarah was there, on the side, jumping up and down. As he came off the court, she threw her arms around his neck and— Wait a minute, what was he thinking? That wasn't the idea at all.

But he had liked thinking about that, too. Nutty was surprised at himself. Really surprised.

CHAPTER SIX

Nutty was a little nervous when he got to the game the next morning. It was the early game, nine o'clock, so not many people were around. A few parents, looking anything but excited, were sitting on the sidelines. Even the referees looked only half awake.

The boys shot the ball around a little, and did a couple of William's passing and lay-up drills. They kept checking out the guys at the other end of the floor, in the bright yellow shirts. They were Rhinos, from Reese School. Noodle knew all of them.

"They're not that great," he told Orlando.

"Are they better than us?"

"Sure. But they're not that great."

"Thanks a million, Noodle. I happen to think we're not so bad."

"Really?"

"Shut up, Noodle."

Nutty was trying not to hear all this. He was concentrating, and watching the ball . . . miss. He couldn't seem to do it this morning. He could see another disaster coming.

The timekeeper was a little late setting things up, so the game was slow getting started, which only gave Nutty more time to worry. But eventually Mr. Nutsell called the boys over to the side.

"Okay, we'll be getting going here in a few minutes. I want to say just a few things. Let's put last week out of our minds. Let's not look to anyone else but ourselves." He slammed his fist into the palm of his hand. "Let's find what's inside us, and let's go out there today and show ourselves what we're made of." This required slamming both fists into his chest. "We don't have to prove anything to anyone. We know what we are and what we can be, and it's what we can be that is who we *really* are. The past means nothing to our future, but the future means everything, because we live for what we're becoming. Reach ahead for your greatness, boys, because it's part of what you are, even if it never has seemed to be. Can you see that? Is that something you can understand? Can you—"

"No, sir," Noodle said. "I got lost about halfway through."

"Shut up," Orlando whispered, "or he'll start all over."

And he did.

William interrupted the recitation where the past and future began to merge. "Excuse me, Mr. Nutsell," William said, "I need to take Nutty back to the locker room. I think he has something in his eye."

"Oh—all right. Well, hurry."

Orlando mumbled that he wanted to go too; he had something in his ear. Richie was giggling and Bilbo told him to quiet down, as Mr. Nutsell started his speech for the third time.

When they reached the locker room, William said, "What you have in your eye is entirely too much reality. We need to get you into your state of oneness with the ball."

"You sound like my dad."

"Please. That's not very kind of you to say."

Nutty didn't give that one much thought. He just leaned back as William pulled out the little basketball and began to swing it in front of Nutty's eyes. "You are relaxing, and what you see before you is a ball. And the ball is everything. Nothing else matters. Nothing else *is*. The ball is part of you, and it is under your command. It will do what you see it doing in your mind. It is commanded by your eyes."

Nutty was moving into "the state." It was relaxing, comfortable. The nervousness was being exhaled from him with each breath. His eyes shut and he saw the hoop, watched the ball, and nothing else made any difference. He liked escaping all the fear and worry he had been feeling.

When the boys returned to the court, Mr. Nutsell was pacing up and down. "Is Freddie all right?"

"Oh, sure," William said. "He's fine now."

"I don't know. His eyes look sort of funny. You didn't put anything in them did you?"

"Of course not."

Nutty was hearing all this as though over a telephone—long distance. He picked up a ball, touched the rough texture, liked the way it felt. He bounced it, and

then he took a mental shot at the distant basket. The ball
sailed at least sixty feet, in a perfect high arc, and
dropped smoothly through the basket. He liked it. He
wanted to shoot some more.

But a ref was blowing his whistle and the boys were
being waved out onto the floor. Nutty stopped near the
back of the jump circle. One of the guys from Reese
said, "Hey, Noodle, don't get sweaty or you'll go limp."

Orlando couldn't pass that one up. "Hey, shorty," he
said, "you'd better watch your mouth or we'll cut Noodle
in half and let him double-team you."

The kid, who was about the same size as Orlando,
tried desperately to think of something to say but managed only an "Oh, yeah?"

But Nutty heard none of this—or that is to say, he
heard it outside. He knew everything that was going on;
he just didn't care. He wanted the ball; he wanted to
shoot. That was all that mattered.

The ref tossed the ball up, but Noodle didn't get the
jump. That was mainly because Noodle, no matter how
hard he tried, could never get both feet off the floor at
the same time. But all that was unimportant to Nutty. He
moved back on defense, guarded his man, waited. He
wanted the ball.

The guard from Reese tried to pass the ball inside
to his center, and Bilbo knocked it away. Orlando picked
it up, and everyone started the other way. Nutty felt the
flow and moved down the court. He stopped near the
top of the key and waited for the ball. Orlando passed it
to him.

Nutty dribbled twice, felt the rightness of everything, moved from floor to air, lofted the ball, and
watched it swoop into the net. From somewhere he had

heard some words: "Work it in. Don't shoot, Freddie, don't shoot—great shot! Way to go." They were all just sounds lying on the edges of his brain. It was the ball he liked, and the swish of the net strings.

Nutty moved back to the other end of the court. This time the guard from Reese made a good pass to the center, who passed off to a forward in the corner. The kid took a shot that bounced long off the rim and Bilbo hardly had to move to get the rebound. Back the other way, flowing.

Nutty waved for the ball, got it in the same spot. Dribbled twice. Up. Floating, watching the ball. Pop. "Nice shooting, Nutty," people were yelling. Nutty had to smile. They didn't know. They didn't understand what was happening. They didn't know the ball the way he did.

And it kept going that way. Nutty shot every time he got his hands on the ball. As the defense moved out, he had to take longer shots; every time, his dad would yell not to shoot and then scream with joy when the ball went in. Nutty made eight straight baskets, and the score was 16 to 4 before the other coach called a time-out.

Nutty didn't want to go to the side. There were too many distractions over there. And then everyone was pounding him on the back. "Nutty, what's gotten into you?" Orlando was saying. "I can't believe those shots you're hitting."

Nutty started to laugh. He looked at Orlando, saw how amazed he was. It was incredible to be so good. He had always wanted to be a good athlete, and now he really was. "Thanks, guys," he was saying. "I guess I'm just hot."

"Okay, Freddie," Dad was saying, "you've been listening to me. You've built up that old confidence, and you know what you can do. I knew this was going to happen. The only thing is, you're shooting from awfully far out. You ought to pass off sometimes too. The other team will probably come out and guard you closer. So don't shoot quite so much."

"All right," Nutty was saying. He was really starting to feel the excitement. They could actually win a game—and not even by forfeit.

When the boys got back out on the floor, Nutty was jumping up and down. He wanted to shoot the ball again, no matter what his dad said. And the first time he got the ball, he really let fly with it. It was a bomb, from almost half court, and it dropped like a bomb—about three feet short of the basket. Nutty was embarrassed. Orlando yelled at him to lay off.

Nutty wanted all the more to prove to himself that he still had his stuff. But Orlando wouldn't pass to him. He brought the ball down and passed to Noodle, who dropped it on the floor. The big center from Reese grabbed it and passed down the court to a guard who had broken behind Nutty. The kid scored an easy lay-up.

The next several times down the floor, Orlando avoided Nutty, and the rest of the team managed to throw the ball away. When Nutty finally got a long rebound, he kept the ball himself, dribbled down the floor, pulled up outside, and let fly with another shot. Nutty wasn't going to let it be short this time. But he threw up a line drive that smashed against the backboard so hard the whole gym rattled.

William called time-out without even asking Mr. Nutsell whether it was all right. And then he said, "I think Nutty still has something in his eye. I'd better have another look."

"I don't know about his eyes. I think he's lost his mind. I'm taking him out of the game until he's ready to pass the ball."

William marched Nutty off to the locker room again. He gave Nutty a rather strong chewing out about letting his success get to him and losing his concentration, and then he got out his gold basketball and started the whole process over. Nutty slipped away quickly this time. He was only too happy to escape the feelings that had been coming on, the nervousness and the embarrassment. It was better to be with the ball, just to concentrate on it, than to get so involved with the outside world.

When Nutty returned to the sideline, he felt right again. But Mr. Nutsell wasn't ready to put him back in. He let Nutty's substitute, Mirkle, play the rest of the half, and by then the score was 24 to 20, Reese ahead.

The other players were very upset during the half-time break, but Nutty didn't think about the score. He thought about the ball and the basket. Some of the guys were now on his back for taking all those long shots. Orlando told him, "Look, you made a few long ones. You got lucky. But don't start that stuff again. Work the ball in."

Mr. Nutsell gave a talk about the true meaning of teamwork. The theme was the same as usual, but this time the main idea was that every truly great human being who had ever lived had learned to be great by playing team sports. Noodle thought he could think of a few exceptions, but Mr. Nutsell ignored the boy completely. Nutty hardly heard any of this, but then, neither did most of the boys.

When they went back out, Nutty was in sync again. He shot whenever he got a chance, from almost anywhere on the floor. He dribbled in close when he could, satisfying some sense that it was what his teammates—and his dad—felt comfortable with. But it really didn't matter. The ball was on an arching wire from his eye to the hoop. It didn't know how to miss.

By the end of the third quarter Reese was buried. Nutty had scored another twenty-two points. But something new was beginning to happen. The Reese players, usually two of them, were coming out to Nutty, guarding him no matter how far he got from the basket. A couple of times he missed shots, when the ball was deflected or his vision at the moment of the shot was blocked. That was frustrating to Nutty. Why did things have to get between him and his basket?

Toward the end, the Reese players were all over him, and Nutty made some bad shots. Finally William suggested it was time he rest. Reese made a run at the Labradors after that, but it was too little too late. The lab school won 54 to 35. Nutty had made forty-one of the points for his team, and most of the shots had been from more than twenty feet away.

But to Nutty it didn't really sink in. He was still in a daze. And then, after the game, the father of one of the Reese kids came over. He had been yelling all through the game, Nutty now remembered.

"Hey, what's the story here?" the man said, and he looked ready to fight someone. "That ain't no fifth-grade kid. What's he doing throwin' the ball from half court like that? That ain't fair."

Mr. Nutsell said, "That's my son. He is a fifth grader, and he's finally gotten in touch with himself, acquired the confidence he's always lacked, and—"

"Don't give me that. The kid has no right to be in a regular kids' league like this."

But then someone else, behind Nutty, said, "I've never seen anything like it in my life. Not in college. Not in pro ball. Not anywhere." It was one of the referees. "What's that kid's name?"

Nutty grinned. He was a hero. An actual, no-question-about-it hero. And now that he was slipping back into the real world, he liked the feeling—liked it a lot.

CHAPTER SEVEN

All weekend Nutty listened to Dad brag about what he had done for Nutty, about Nutty's certain full scholarship to a major college, about his NBA career. Mom just kept laughing. She seemed to think the game had been some sort of fluke. As for Nutty, he hardly knew what to think of it all. The truth was, he really couldn't remember much about the game.

But Monday morning was a whole new thing. The word spread fast, and everyone was coming up to Nutty, asking whether he really scored forty-one points. The only ones who didn't were the kids who had heard he had scored sixty or eighty. "I hear you were shooting from *everywhere*, and you just couldn't miss. Is that right?" He heard that sort of question dozens of times, and he just kept saying, "I guess I got kind of hot. I was probably just lucky."

Mrs. Ash stopped him in the hallway and said, "You're the hero of the school, Nutty. Everyone's talking about you. Did you guys really win a game?"

"Yeah, we won."

"And how many points did you score?"

"I don't remember exactly. I think it was maybe forty-one, or something like that."

The truth was, Nutty was loving all the attention. But he was kind of scared too. Maybe he couldn't do it again. Maybe he had gotten in that one groove, where everything worked, but would get nervous next week and be unable to shoot like that. William said that's why even the greatest players didn't stay hot. They let their minds interfere. Nutty wasn't sure whether or not his would do the same.

At lunch, with Bilbo and Richie and Orlando, Nutty noticed something else that made him worry. "Hello, gunner," Orlando said. His voice was playful, but "gunner" was not exactly what Nutty wanted to be called.

Nutty just set his tray down and then said, "I think I blew that math test. How did you guys do?"

"I got them all right," Bilbo said. He was looking at a gob of something with noodles in it, a casserole of some sort, as though he still hadn't made up his mind to give it a try. "This stuff looks like Nodel's legs."

"How could you do well in math, Nutty?" Orlando said. "You spent all last week practicing basketball."

"Well, it worked," Richie said. "Geez, Nutty, you were fantastic. My dad was at the game, and he's never seen even a pro hit that many outside shots. He kept talking about it all weekend."

"I do need to spend more time on my math."

"Come on, Nutty," Orlando said. "Please don't be humble. I'd rather hear you brag than pretend you're not thinking how great you are."

"Maybe that's not what I'm thinking."

"Oh, sure. Nutty, have you ever heard of passing the ball? That's what you do in basketball. Bilbo is one of our best players, and he hardly took a shot. His only chance to touch the ball was when he got a rebound."

"Hey, listen," Bilbo said. "I shot four times and made one basket. Nutty was hitting everything from everywhere. Why shouldn't he do the shooting?"

Orlando let the whole thing drop for the moment, but Nutty could see some problems coming. Orlando was not happy, and Nutty knew no one else would be if he continued to do all the shooting. He tried again to get to some other subject.

"Student Council meeting is coming up this week," Nutty said. "Do any of you guys have anything you want brought up?"

"Yeah," Orlando said. "What about this slimy stuff they're feeding us? It looks like something my dog was eating the other day—for the second time."

"Come on, Orlando," Richie said, "don't be so gross. I'm trying to eat the stuff."

"Nutty was supposed to improve the lunches. Remember?"

"Orlando," Bilbo said. "You know as well as I do that Dr. Dunlop keeps promising and then not doing anything. Nutty can't help that." Bilbo was a good friend, Nutty decided.

"I don't see why not. When he was elected, he told everybody—"

"Orlando, I won't shoot so much next week. Okay?"

"What?"

"I know you're mad at me for shooting so much. I got hot, and I just couldn't resist. But I know I took too many shots."

"If you do all the shooting, they'll only guard you."

"I know. That's right. I'm not a very good passer, and all my shots were going in, so I just kept shooting."

Suddenly Orlando started to laugh and the tension was broken. "The guy can't pass, so he throws the ball into the basket. Could someone tell me how that makes sense?"

Nutty managed to get the subject changed again. He really was feeling strange about all this. He had wanted to shoot better, but he hadn't thought much about how the others, especially Orlando, might feel about it.

After the boys had eaten a little—that is to say, as much as they could stand—they took their trays to the front, and then they headed for the cafeteria exit. But Orlando took hold of Nutty's arm and stopped him, letting the others go on ahead.

"Listen, Nutty, maybe you've got all those other guys fooled, but I know something's going on."

"Going on? What are you talking about?"

"I know you, Nutty. You can't shoot like that. Nobody can get that good that fast."

"I practiced." Nutty tried to walk away, but Orlando still had hold of his arm.

"Hey, who do you think you're talking to? I've been shooting baskets with you since we were about seven. You never made two shots in a row before in your life."

"Well, I'm getting better." Nutty was tempted to tell the truth, but William had told him not to.

"William is behind this, Nutty. I know he is. He was over at your house every day last week. He took you into the locker room just before the game, and you came out looking like you were in some other world. Then, when you finally missed a couple of shots, when you started playing the way you usually do, he took you out again. You came back with that look in your eyes and during the whole second half you threw in almost everything you shot."

"He's been helping me concentrate. It makes a big difference."

"Come on, Nutty. There's got to be more to it than that."

"Not really. I don't know what else to tell you."

"I want in on it. I want to shoot like that too."

Nutty suddenly realized something else about himself. He didn't want to tell Orlando, and it wasn't only because of William.

"Look, Orlando, there's no big secret. If you concentrate when you shoot, it really helps. Everyone knows that."

Orlando was not satisfied, but he also seemed unsure what else to say. He was looking hard at Nutty, still seeming skeptical, when a voice came from behind them.

"Hi, Nutty."

Nutty twisted to look. It was Sarah. "Oh, hi." Nutty turned toward her, happy for the escape, but also rather self-conscious.

"Wow, I heard about the game. You're turning into some kind of superstar."

"Oh, brother," Orlando moaned, and he walked away.

"Not really," Nutty said. "I just had a good day, I guess." Sarah had on a blue shirt, and it made her eyes bluer than ever. There was something about that playful smile, and her nose that turned up just a little, and her long brown hair—something that . . . something that Nutty really didn't want to think about.

"You had more than a good day. From what I heard, you were great."

"I just got hot, I guess."

"Hottest guy around," she said, and she winked.

She did. She actually winked at him. Nutty's heart was suddenly doing *ka-boom-ka-booms*. Since when did she say stuff like that to guys? He had known her all her life and she had never once . . .

"Do you want to play basketball in high school and college?"

"I guess so. I haven't thought much about it."

"I want to start coming to your games now, but I have gymnastics at the same time. Maybe sometime I'll take a day off and come to a game."

"Yeah, well, that'd be great if you came to see me . . . or, I mean, us."

She winked again—just barely, just enough so that he was hardly sure it had happened. Was she really doing that on purpose? She had always been friendly, but she had never . . . flirted. Was that what she was doing? "It's you I want to watch," she said, and she gave him a sly little smile and walked away.

Nutty was trying to remember where he was and where he was going. And then he heard laughter behind him. Bilbo and Richie had come back, looking for him.

"Oh, Nutty, it's *you* I want to watch," Bilbo said.

"Be quiet," Nutty said, embarrassed. Maybe Bilbo wasn't such a great friend after all.

"Well," Richie said, in a deep, faked voice, "I know I'm a great hero, but I'd be even better with you watching me, Sarah, my little sweety-poo."

Nutty fought not to laugh.

"Oh, you're my hero, Nutty Nutsell. You're so good you're bad."

Nutty started to move away now, heading to class.

"Wouldn't you just love me in a cute little cheerleader outfit, Nutty my love?"

"I mean it, you guys. Lay off."

"Oh, Nutty, you can't miss—not the basket and not my tender little heart."

"I'm serious, guys. I want you to get off my case." But Nutty was grinning, no matter how mad he was trying to sound.

And Richie got in the last word before Nutty walked into class. "Well, Sarah, my sweet thing, I'm sure I'd be ever so much better—even though I don't have much room for improvement—if you would give me a big smooch for luck."

Nutty sat down at his desk, still grinning, and then he said, "lay off," one more time. Except now he was talking to himself, to that stupid heart of his that had decided on its own to start pounding like it was a bass drum.

CHAPTER EIGHT

When William got home from school that afternoon, Nutty was waiting. William had to take a bus every day to the private school he attended, and he was always a little late getting home. As he came strolling up the street, he seemed lost in thought, as always, and he was halfway up the front walk before he even noticed Nutty sitting on his steps. Nutty couldn't believe what William was wearing: The wool scarf was bad enough, but earmuffs? Who else would wear earmuffs?

"Ah, Nutty, what are you doing?"

"Freezing my behind off. What does it look like?"

"You should dress warmer. You need some nice earmuffs, like mine." He chuckled. He obviously knew what Nutty would think of the things. "Why didn't you go inside?"

"Because your mother would make a big fuss and give me cocoa to drink, and all that kind of stuff."

"Yes, yes. She would at that. Actually, I don't think she's home anyway. She meets with her literary club on Mondays."

William had a key. In fact, for some reason, he had a whole ringful of keys. He fumbled around, trying to get the right one without taking off his mittens. At last he got the door open.

The boys went to William's bedroom, where William began to strip off layers of clothes. He had on a sweater under the big coat. "Take off your coat, Nutty. I can almost guess what you want to talk to me about."

Nutty slipped off his coat. "Who are all those guys?" he said. He was pointing to a row of pictures over William's desk.

"Ah, I'm glad you noticed. I got those for Christmas, and just got around to putting them up." He pointed to each in turn. "That's Aristotle, Bacon, Hobbes, Descartes, Spinoza, and Leibnitz—some of my heroes. They're all philosophers." He chuckled again. "Have you put up a collection of basketball players on your walls by now?"

"No, I haven't."

"I think I catch a little something in your voice. I think I know what's going on. I suspected it would set in by now."

"What are you talking about?"

"I'm only guessing, of course, but I suspect all the attention was somewhat difficult to handle today, once the initial pleasure of it wore off. More important, I suspect that your friends are less than thrilled with your newfound capacities."

"Not all of them. Mainly—"

"Orlando."

"How did you know that?"

"Orlando considers himself an athlete. He consistently overrates his innate abilities. It cannot be easy for him to see you excel when he is, sad to say, mediocre."

"But that's just the thing. Why can't we—"

"You want me to share our techniques with the whole team, of course. You find yourself feeling guilty about having a secret that you haven't shared with your best friends, especially when it sets you clearly above them. Is that about it?"

"Not about. That's it. Except—"

"Except that you also would like to keep it to yourself, because you do enjoy the attention, after all, even if you have complex feelings about it. And of course, that also makes you feel guilty."

"Yeah. Something like that. Except I thought I was just all mixed-up. You probably understand me better than I do."

"It would not be the first time," William said, with that knowing smile of his. "But let me take some of the guilt off you. It's my technique. I taught it to you. And I told you not to share it. Not only that, I continue to refuse to teach anyone else. So all that is my fault, and you can't help it."

"Why won't you teach anyone else?"

"Nutty, we jumped into this whole thing without giving enough thought to the implications. I was so enthusiastic about the possibilities that I didn't consider the realities. Yesterday and today I've seen a much larger picture, and I now know that we've opened up, as they say, a real can of worms. We have challenged the accepted norms of athletic perfection, and in the process, we just may be threatening the meaning of sport itself."

"Come on, William, don't talk like a philosopher. Just tell me what you're talking about."

"Fine. Consider the following: Number one, we understand little about the emotional implications of my method. The trancelike state may have psychological effects that we have no way of predicting.

"Number two, we could destroy the whole game of basketball and most other sports. If people never miss, why play? Competition loses all meaning.

"Number three, if this system works as well as we suspect, you could be recruited by pros before you even enter adolescence. That would be tempting, but perhaps not the best thing for you.

"And number four, even more worrisome, I could be the one recruited to teach my methods, and you would be just another perfect shooter. Not to mention that my life was never intended to be wasted on athletics."

"Oh, wow, William. How do you get me into things like this?"

"I believe *you* called me." William leaned back, patted his stomach, and enjoyed his own "joke." Nutty saw nothing funny in it. But just as suddenly, William was serious again. "In any case, let's experiment with the thing a little more and see how it goes. I simply can't resist finding out what we really have here. But no matter what, do not tell anyone what's going on."

"I told Orlando that you were teaching me to concentrate."

"Good. That's true, and yet it avoids the deeper implications of what we're doing. As you must also realize by now, this system does have some practical problems I hadn't foreseen. The fact is, close guarding and double-teaming may keep you from doing so well as we thought."

"Yeah, what are we going to do about that?" Nutty knew that he did want to keep shooting well, even if he was worried about what might come of it.

"Well, I've been thinking about that too. We worked only on your shooting. Now we need to make you the best passer around, a pinpoint passer who can spot the man left open and deliver the assist. This will solve several problems. First, your teammates will feel better about you. Second, the defense will have to drop back to guard the other boys, or at least one of them will. And third, if you're one-on-one, you should be able to get open at times to take that perfect shot of yours. You do, after all, enjoy making it, I believe." That knowing smile of his returned.

"I don't know whether I enjoy it or not. During the game I hardly knew what I was doing. I felt like I was in a dream."

"Is that so? Well, that's a factor we'll have to consider as we go along. Should we begin our imaging? I'll get my little basketball and we can get busy on your passing game."

William got up from his chair and walked over to a chest of drawers. Nutty moved over to the bed, where he could lie down and start his envisioning. But as William approached, Nutty said, "William, if I get to be a good basketball player, it's because of you, not me."

"Ah, the other issue. I knew that would come up too, but I did not wish to seem arrogant enough to suggest it." He sat down, crossed his arms, and then lifted one hand to his chin. "Every athlete has a coach. It's as simple as that. The teacher shares in the glory, but still, the athlete performs and so, rightly, receives the most attention."

"But maybe this is more than that. Maybe I'm not even doing it. When I was my regular self, I couldn't hit a thing."

"No, no. There aren't two people. There are merely the concentrating Nutty and the nonconcentrating Nutty. But when all is said and done, *you* do the concentrating—and the shooting. I don't."

Nutty wasn't sure about that, but he let it go. He really did want to feel that he was getting to be good at the game.

"Now, is there anything else you need to talk about, or think through? Let's clear your mind, or you won't be able to reach the complete state of concentration you need for this new skill."

"I'm ready," Nutty said, and he waited for the swinging little ball, but just as William suspended it before his eyes, Nutty said, "Maybe there is one other thing."

"Yes. And what is that?"

"Well, this is something off the subject."

"That's fine. Let's take care of it."

"It's just something I'm sort of curious about, not anything, you know, really important or anything like that."

"That's fine. What is it?"

"I was wondering when most guys started to . . . or, I mean, I've been thinking about . . . I don't exactly mean *thinking* about, but I've been wondering about the subject—what I mean is— Oh, never mind."

"No, no. Come clean, now. What subject are you referring to?"

"Well, uh . . . girls."

"Oh, dear," William said, and he stood up. "This could add a whole new dimension to our project."

"No, no. I'm not interested in girls myself. I just wondered when most guys started to be, and what they did about it, and . . . Actually I don't know what I was thinking. Let's just drop the whole thing."

"Who is she?"

"No. Really. I don't—"

"I think it's best if you tell me, Nutty."

Nutty really didn't like this at all. And yet, he wanted to talk to someone. "It's Sarah Montag. I think she was flirting with me today. Maybe she sort of liked me before, but now that I did well in basketball I think she likes me even more."

"Yes, yes. That's part of our culture. The brawny athlete is still very much the desirable male. I'm afraid the mind and the intellect never will receive fair respect."

"So what do I do?"

"Do?"

"Yeah. I don't want to have a girlfriend or anything. I don't really want her to like me, I don't think. It would make things too complicated."

"Well, then, I see no problem. Just forget her. In a few years, you'll have plenty of time for all that."

"Yeah, but something's going on."

"Going on?"

"Yeah. The other night I was thinking about shooting the ball, and making baskets, and I was trying just to concentrate on the basket, and then I started thinking about everyone thinking I was good, and then, the next thing I knew I was thinking about . . . her."

"Oh, dear. That is a problem."

"Do you think so?"

"Nutty, I've not looked into these matters thoroughly, but I suspect this is a rather juvenile form of what is traditionally called love."

"Love?" Nutty sat up. "Wait a minute, William. All I did was think about her for a couple of seconds—or maybe thirty. I didn't—"

"Yes, but the connection of glory and attention to a particular female would seem to be an indication of an innocent, and yet perhaps intense, attachment. It is the first stirring of adolescence in you, Nutty. I suppose it's inevitable."

"I don't want to be in love, William. I've never been interested in that kind of stuff."

William thought for a moment. "Why don't you just lie back and tell me what you think about when you think of her. Envision her, and then report your emotions."

Nutty lay back down, shut his eyes, and he saw her smiling at him in that sly way and winking. "I keep seeing her mouth, William, and I like it. And her nose too. I never liked anyone's nose before."

"Oh, dear."

"And I get sort of tense all over and nervous from having her looking at me, and I want to run and I want to stay at the same time."

"Oh, dear."

"But I don't like it. That's a good sign, isn't it?"

"Hardly. It fits the whole pattern. From all I know on the subject of love, you really have little chance of getting out of this situation without a certain amount of pain."

"Oh, wow," Nutty said. "I had a feeling it was going to be something like that. What do I do?"

"You're asking *me*? Nutty, you're entirely out of my area of expertise this time."

"Oh, brother. Then I'm in real trouble."

CHAPTER NINE

The next three Saturdays were great triumphs for Nutty and the Labradors. In each game Nutty hit all his shots until the opposing coach started sending two and three guys out to guard him, and as soon as that happened, Nutty started passing off. He was still not a great dribbler, but when he saw an extra defender coming in on him, he would spot the open player and drill him with a pass. The other guys still missed plenty of shots, but Nutty was pulling the defense so far away from the basket that his own teammates had a good chance of getting the rebound and shooting again.

Orlando was definitely improving too. He had never practiced so hard in his life. He actually was more of a ball handler than Nutty, and he was quicker, too. He was getting to be one of the better players in the league. All the same, he was frustrated. Crowds were starting to show up at the games—and they were *not* coming to see Orlando.

At first only kids from the lab school came to the games, and a few parents; but an article in the local paper, and then one in Kansas City, began to bring out some real crowds. Both articles said basically the same thing: A fifth-grade kid in Warrensburg, Missouri, *can't miss.*

A lot of people wanted to see that. Most of them entered the gym rather skeptical about the whole thing—and left in awe. A television crew from Kansas City showed up at the fifth game, and afterward a guy Nutty had seen on the television sports news stuck a microphone in Nutty's face and began asking a lot of questions. It was hard for Nutty to think for a while after a game. He was still in his own world. "I just try to do my best," he told the man, and he answered every question with more or less the same response.

The local high-school coach, who had attended the fourth game as well, came over to talk to Nutty as soon as the camera crew was finished. "Young man," he said, shaking his head as though he couldn't think what to say, "I've never seen anything like that."

Nutty was still pretty much in his distant state. He just nodded.

"I understand you're also the Student Council president at school."

"Yes, sir."

"Are you a good student?"

"Pretty good, I guess."

"Well, you'll have no trouble getting a college scholarship. The only thing is, there may not be much point in playing college ball when you could go straight to the pros and become a millionaire."

Mr. Nutsell was standing behind Nutty. He had been saying how proud he was of his boy, and then he heard "millionaire." "Excuse me," he said, "I'm Coach Nutsell. I'm Freddie's father. Do you really think he could play pro ball?"

The high-school coach was a big man, even taller than Mr. Nutsell and twice as thick through the chest. He reached out and put a hand on Nutty's shoulder, but he looked at Mr. Nutsell. "Are you kidding? I've never seen a shooter like this *anywhere.*"

"Well, I know he's been really hot these last few games, but I just thought—"

"Hot? He wasn't hot today. I've never seen a kid this young—much less a high-school or college player—as cool as he is. He just goes up and pops that jumper and runs away. He knows it's going in. I didn't see one sign that he was even feeling anything. Those kids were all over him, and he never once got rattled."

"Well, that's true. He has developed a lot of self-control lately—at least when he's playing basketball."

"Listen, Mr. Nutsell, keep this kid healthy. I can't wait to get him at the high school. I'm even going to see what the rules are about junior-high kids playing high-school ball. I'll tell you, you've got yourself a gold mine. Whatever you're doing with him, just keep it up."

"Well, you know, I've done a lot of work with the boys on their attitudes. I've talked to them about believing in themselves and reaching inside and really—"

"Yeah, well, we all shovel some of that stuff in this business. But the main thing is, the kid can shoot the basketball—and you've done a pretty nice job with your offensive design too. It's really built to take advantage of what your boy does."

Mr. Nutsell thanked the coach, but he glanced over at William, who, Nutty noticed, was trying to act as though he hadn't heard. Nonetheless, he was smiling just a bit and Nutty knew he was enjoying all this.

And so was Nutty—some. But not enough. He had always dreamed of being a basketball player, a real star at the high school maybe. He imagined the crowds cheering and everyone slapping him on the back when he hit a crucial shot to win a big game. But what was happening now just wasn't like that at all.

After the games, when people talked to him about what he had done, it seemed as though they were talking about someone else: some hero out of a movie, some fiction. The games themselves were really quite boring. He would drop back on defense, guard his man, and then, once his team had the ball, move up the floor, usually take a pass from Orlando and, if he was open, go up for the shot—which would go in. If he was covered, he passed off. That was all there was. Plus, everything took place in a gray sort of numbness that came over him as he stared at the little basketball and listened to William's voice, and that numbness didn't wear off until some time after the final score was posted. In the first few games he had liked the peace and unity he felt with the ball, but now the whole thing was becoming routine.

Nutty thanked the coach and walked toward the locker room. But everyone wanted to get close to Nutty, touch him, congratulate him. A lot of the kids from school were there, and they were all raving about how great he was. Nutty kept saying thank you, and he kept fighting to come back into the real world. It was not easy.

It was like shaking off sleep on a dark, cold winter morning when the warm covers seemed more inviting.

In the locker room the guys were surprisingly quiet. They weren't whooping and celebrating the way they had after their first couple of wins. Nutty sat down and started to take off his shoes.

"What's the matter?" Bilbo said. He had already showered, and he was getting dressed now. He sat down next to Nutty.

"Nothing."

"You act weird during these games, Nutty—and afterward, too. I noticed it earlier in the season, but it's getting worse with each game."

"He says he has to concentrate," Orlando said. There was an edge of sarcasm in his voice.

"Nutty," Bilbo said, "everybody on the team says that William's been giving you special help and that's why you're doing so great."

Nutty didn't know what to say. He didn't want to lie, but William kept saying not to tell anyone what they had been doing.

"They get together almost every night," Orlando said. "William's teaching him some kind of stuff that makes him shoot like that. But he's not about to let the rest of us in on it. He wants to be the big hero."

When Nutty still didn't comment, Bilbo said, "Lay off, Orlando. First you said he wouldn't pass the ball, and that's what made you mad. Now he passes all the time, but you're still mad because he shoots better than you do. The problem with you is, you're just jealous."

"Hey, I scored almost as many points as he did today."

"Yeah," Richie said, "and you took five times as many shots."

"I didn't see *you* doing anything. Were you even out there?"

"Lay off," Bilbo said again. "Richie hardly gets a chance. You hog the ball all the time."

"I do not. What are you talking about?"

"Yeah, you do," Noodle said. "You shot the ball every time you got near it. I was wide open under the basket about ten times, and you wouldn't pass to me."

"Why should I? You can't even make a lay-up, for crying out loud." Orlando was shouting now.

"Orlando, would you—"

"Don't, you guys." Nutty had spoken in that calm, distant voice. There was something strange and eerie about it.

The room was quiet for several seconds, and then Bilbo said, "Nutty, something's wrong with you. You're acting really weird."

Nutty looked at Bilbo. Gradually, he was starting to feel some emotion, some clarity again. "I'm okay," he said. "But let's not get on each other. Let's just have fun. Hey, we really racked those guys. Are we bad, or what?"

Orlando laughed in his familiar way, that mischievous tone returning. "Hey, you know what one of the Southeast guys said to me? It was when we were ahead by about thirty, and they were getting more and more messed up. We were getting ready for a foul shot. And he looked over and said, 'We beat you guys easy last year.' He sounded like he was about ready to start crying."

"What did you say to him?" Noodle asked.

Orlando laughed. "I tried to give him some good advice. I said, 'Son, you can't live in the past.'"

The guys liked that; they all laughed. Bilbo said, "That young man needs to hear one of Mr. Nutsell's talks. He needs to reach inside himself and find out what he's made of."

"That's the trouble," Orlando said. "He reached inside and got hold of something soft and squishy. Now he thinks he's a loser."

Nutty smiled; he wanted to laugh, but he couldn't quite manage it.

That evening Nutty was on the TV news. He watched himself, unbelieving. He had no idea he looked like that. He was hitting those long shots and making great passes, and it was like watching some athlete at the Olympics and wondering how he ever got so good.

Mom had started coming to the games, but Susie still hadn't been to any. She had made fun of all the fuss about Nutty. But now, as she watched on television, her mouth was wide open. "How can you do that?" she kept saying.

Nutty didn't answer. He was listening to the announcer: "I'll tell you—this kid defies description. I wouldn't have believed it if I hadn't seen it. He missed only three shots in the whole game, and he canned nineteen, most of them from *way* outside. When he wasn't doing that, he was threading the needle with passes to the open man—or I should say kid, because the rest of the players shoot and play like regular eleven- and twelve-year-old boys. The boy they call Nutty—Freddie Nutsell—belongs to some other league. But then, there

may not be a tough-enough league for him anywhere
. . . at least not on this planet. The kid is simply unreal."

That's right, I am, Nutty said to himself, but he
wasn't sure what he meant.

"My goodness," Mom was saying. "This is all a little
too much to accept. I can hardly—"

"Oh, honey, don't talk that way," Mr. Nutsell said.
"The potential of the human being is so much greater
than we ever imagine. Most people never unleash the
power within themselves. I've talked to Freddie a lot,
and I think he's finally gotten in touch with that power.
It's really not that mysterious when you look at it from
that point of view."

Nutty got up and walked into the kitchen to call
William. "Did you see the news?" he said.

"Certainly."

"William, I feel a little strange about all this."

"Strange? Why?"

"It's not even me."

"Don't start that again, Nutty."

"What if people start figuring out what's going on?"

"Nothing's going on. We're not cheating. We've just
improved your concentration."

"Well, what do I say to people when they ask why I
got better so fast?"

"Tell them the truth."

"The truth? Really?"

"Sure. Just say, 'I've worked on my concentration,
and that's really helped.'"

"What about the trance, and the gold basketball and
all that?"

"Well, you needn't go into any details."

CHAPTER TEN

The next game was a rematch against Ridge View. The Raiders had not yet lost a game. The Labradors needed to beat them to move into a tie for first. The guys on the team were not really worried that they could do it, but they were excited before the game, partly because they wanted revenge and partly because of all the razzing they had been taking from the Ridge View players since the first game.

When Nutty walked into the gym, before he even had a chance to go into the locker room and get dressed, the big guy on the Raider team, Erin, walked over and said, "So, is this the hot shot who gets himself on TV?" Erin looked more like a high-school kid than a fifth grader; a lot of kids claimed he had flunked a few times.

Nutty kept walking.

"Hey, Nutty, you may have fooled those guys from Channel Five, but you can't fool us. We know you."

To Nutty this was all just talk. Most of the guys from Ridge View had been at the Labradors' last game, since it was right after their own. They had seen what Nutty had done.

"Maybe you won't be so great if someone who can guard gets on you."

"Maybe not," Nutty said, and he smiled.

This only made Erin angry. "You just wait and see what happens today. The first time you try one of your cute little jump shots in front of me, you're going to be on your rear end."

Nutty stopped. He leaned forward and looked very closely at the guy's face, studying it. At last he said, "You may land on yours too. Or you may land on your face. But I'm not sure how I'll know which is which—since the two look so much alike."

"Hey." The kid reached for Nutty's shirt, but Nutty stepped back quickly and then walked away. "You just wait, little Nutty. You're going to *pay* for that one."

But Nutty, for some reason, felt better than he had in weeks. He went into the locker room laughing, and told Orlando, "Let's murder these guys, all right?"

"All *right*," Orlando said, and he looked happier too. "I'm going to show some *moves* to that kid they had on me last time." He pretended to dribble, bouncing the imaginary ball between his legs and behind his back. "I'm not saying I'll be good. It's *great* we're talking here today."

"You won't have to be," Bilbo said. "After all the press Nutty's been getting, the whole team will be guarding him. All we'll have to do is our lay-up drills."

And that's how the guys felt when they went out on the floor to warm up. The Raiders kept up the chatter and insults, and the Labradors answered primarily with knowing smiles. They were going to *kill* these guys. But Nutty had told the players on his team what he had said about Erin's face, and Orlando finally couldn't help rubbing that one in.

"Hey, Erin," he yelled, "I think you put your trunks on wrong. You're mooning everyone."

Erin stopped and pointed. "You're going to get it too."

Nutty was about to yell something at Erin, tell him what he thought of him, when William called him over. It was time to go in and get Nutty into the right mental state. Although Nutty knew he had to do it, he hated the thought. He was having too much fun.

But once the little ball started to swing and William's calming voice took over, Nutty's emotions slipped away, and the numb feeling engulfed him. When he came back out, he was again in that strange world where nothing but the ball existed and everything hovered round him like shadows at dusk. He began to shoot his perfect jump shots. Some of the Ridge View guys were still yelling insults, but none of that truly registered now. Nutty heard very few sounds, either inside or outside his head. All was visual—the ball, the hoop—except for the feel of things: the snap of his wrist, the calm assurance in his head, in his whole body.

The Labradors really got after Ridge View when the game started. They were playing much better defense than they had early in the season. William had taught them a switching defense, sometimes using a zone, and then coming out into man-to-man. The lab school boys were smaller, but they were aggressive, and they were doing some excellent ball hawking.

Just as expected, however, Nutty had two players on him wherever he went. And these guys were guarding close, pushing and shoving. In the first quarter, the only shots Nutty took were foul shots, all of which he sank. Erin was guarding Bilbo, so he hadn't been able to get close to Nutty, but he was still making threats whenever he had a chance. The idea seemed to be that such talk would rattle Nutty, but so far, nothing had gotten through to him.

Nutty did a good job of passing off, and many times Orlando just brought the ball down and fed the open man while two guys were occupied with Nutty. This led to some easy lay-ups, and the Raiders were getting behind. They were also getting frustrated.

When Nutty stepped to the line for another foul shot, Erin took the position on the line away from the basket. He normally was closer, where he could use his height to get the rebound. Nutty paid no attention. He shot, and watched the ball drop through the hoop. Then, suddenly, he was on his back. Erin had run right through him, throwing a shoulder into Nutty's chest.

The referees obviously had not seen what happened, and assumed the two had just bumped into each other. But Nutty was slow in getting up, and when he did, he was furious. "Hey, he can't do that," he yelled at the ref.

Mr. Nutsell was also up yelling, but play continued. Nutty ran down the floor, but by then the Raiders had scored. Nutty stopped, and Orlando hit him with a long pass. He was all alone, and he could have gone in for a lay-up, but he pulled up and took his patented long jumper—and missed everything. The ball bounced out of bounds and went over to Ridge View.

Erin ran up behind Nutty and said, "What's the matter? Lose your shooting eye?"

Nutty spun around and was about to punch the guy, when Bilbo grabbed him. "Don't, Nutty. You'll get thrown out."

Nutty pushed Bilbo away, but he agreed, and he tried to settle down. But all this had slowed his getting down court and his man scored. Nutty knew what was happening now, and he took a deep breath, trying to calm himself. He took a pass from Orlando and immediately went up for a shot. Another one of the Raiders smashed into him, sending him flying.

The whistle blew, but Nutty came up ready to fight again. Richie got him this time and had to hang on tight; Nutty was struggling to get away. He was outraged.

The referee was shouting, "All right, that's a flagrant foul. This young man is ejected from the game, and you, Number Twelve, had better calm yourself down or you'll be gone too."

Nutty nodded. He had to get back into himself. He walked to the foul line. But he could hear his heart beating and feel his face burning. Erin walked past Nutty. "We don't care if we lose Hanson. We know you can't play once you get mad—and you're mad, aren't you, twinkle-toes?"

But Nutty wasn't going to lose control. He was going to make the two foul shots. He bounced the ball, breathed deeply, looked at the hoop, and released the ball. It hit hard off the back of the rim—a real brick of a shot—and bounced away. Erin started laughing.

Nutty couldn't help it. He was furious. "Look, Erinboy," he said, and he turned toward Erin. But Bilbo had grabbed Nutty's shirt and was pulling on it. "Time-out, Nutty. Your dad wants to talk to us."

Nutty let himself be pulled a few steps away, and then he walked over to the side. Mr. Nutsell came out halfway to meet him. "Son, son, can't you see what they're trying to do? You can't let them bother you like that."

Nutty was hardly listening. He was noticing the crowd now. A lot of kids were there from both schools, and they were all screaming like crazy. Nutty also saw a row of men, all wearing sweaters. Coaches, he thought. Maybe they were scouting him, trying to see if he really was that great. His stomach was knotting up with nervousness. He had to play better. He couldn't let everyone down.

"Just a minute," he said to his dad, and he pulled away from the grip on his arm and went to William. "Let's go back in the locker room. I need to get back in my . . . you know . . ."

"Get yourself back, Nutty," William said, very calmly. "You need to learn to do that. This is a good chance to find out whether you can."

"I can't, William. I need you to help me concentrate."

"I don't think so. You need to take control of yourself. You can do it."

"Come on, William. Don't mess around. We're going to lose if this keeps up."

But William would not budge, and when the players went back out on the court, Nutty to take his second shot, he was still feeling excited and nervous. As he stepped to the line, Erin said, under his breath, "You're mad, Nutty. You want to kill me, don't you? You can't handle the pressure."

Nutty bounced the ball a couple of times, and then he took two or three deep breaths. And he talked to himself, using William's words. "You and the ball. Only you and the ball . . . and the basket. The ball arches perfectly, guided by your eyes. You cannot miss; your eyes will not let you miss. The ball is under your control; it is part of you. Nothing else exists."

"Let's go, young man." It was the ref, but Nutty barely heard him.

"You cannot miss. The ball does not know how to miss. It is part of you."

Nutty released the ball, felt the snap, and turned before it ever reached the net. He knew it would go in. He couldn't miss.

All was in control again. The Raiders were gambling that Nutty had lost his cool and wouldn't shoot well now. They had only one man on him. Nutty was able to get some shots off, and now he was clicking. Every shot swished the net, not even touching the rim. When the defenders moved in tighter again, double-teaming, Nutty passed off. The rout was on.

Orlando was out there glorying in it somewhere, but Nutty was inside himself, flowing up and down the court, dominating, but not really there. He heard no more insults, didn't even notice the frustration of the Ridge View players.

By the fourth quarter the game was out of reach and Nutty was sitting on the bench. Mr. Nutsell was letting Mirkle and Pandelli and Goutz have a chance to play. Nutty had little to say to the other guys on the bench, who were yelling and celebrating as the final seconds ticked away.

When the game was over Nutty went to the locker room immediately. Bilbo tried to talk to him, but Nutty didn't feel like talking. He really couldn't. The trance was too deep this time, and it didn't want to let go. There was no way he could go back out where all those men would be waiting to talk to him. The next thing he knew he calmly walked over to the window, opened it, and then got up on a bench to climb out. He didn't remember ever deciding to do such a thing; it simply seemed the only thing he could do.

Orlando said, "Nutty, what the heck are you doing?" But Nutty didn't answer. He only knew he wanted to get away.

So Nutty climbed out the window, and he walked home alone. When he got there he was remembering the fight he almost got into. He wished he had punched old Erin and gotten thrown out of the game. He wasn't sure why the idea appealed to him so much, but it did.

He went to his room and sat on his bed, trying to think what to do. Slowly, he was coming back to reality, but it was a little hard to remember how he had gotten home or why he had been so against talking to people. It was all very confusing. Finally he decided he would go out to the back yard and just shoot at his old hoop behind the patio. It was something he hadn't done for a long time.

He had been there only a few minutes when his mom came outside. "Hey, where were you after the game? How did you get away without us?"

"I just wanted to walk."

"What's the matter, honey?"

"Nothing."

"You looked so strange when you were playing, Freddie. You don't seem to be having any fun."

"The idea is to win, not to have fun."

"Do you really believe that?"

Nutty banged a shot off the front of the rim. "I don't know. I know it's fun to win."

"Is it? You didn't look very happy when the game ended."

"I was tired, I guess."

He tried another jump shot, but it was long and bounced away. He ran after the ball, and then he sailed another shot that passed high over the basket.

"What's going on?"

Nutty turned around. His dad was there now. "What?"

"What are you doing?"

"Just shooting. I haven't played basketball for a long time."

"What?"

Nutty suddenly realized what he had said. He grabbed the ball and then he looked at it, as though he didn't recognize what it was.

"Son, you just missed three shots in a row."

"I did, didn't I?" Nutty was stunned.

"You shouldn't just mess around like that, Freddie. You'll get out of your groove."

"Oh, leave him alone," Mom said. "Maybe he *should* get out of whatever this groove is. Maybe he's in too deep."

"There's no such thing."

But Nutty was still staring at the basketball. It was like an old friend he hadn't seen for far too long.

CHAPTER ELEVEN

Nutty always felt quite different about his basketball exploits by Monday. It was as though he had become two people: the basketball player, lost in a trance, and the kid who gradually came back to life as the weekend continued. When he got back to school, everyone made such a huge fuss over him, and he really couldn't help finding pleasure in that—even though he did constantly wonder whether he wasn't a sort of fake. "Nutty couldn't do all this stuff," he told William one night. "It's that other guy who gets in me during the games. To tell the truth, I still think it's you."

But William merely chuckled. "I could concentrate all I wanted, Nutty, but I couldn't shoot a basketball. I lack the basic skill."

Maybe so. In any case, when everyone made such a big deal over him, Nutty was embarrassed, but he loved it too. When Dr. Dunlop stopped him in the hallway and

told him that he always knew Nutty was destined for
great things, Nutty almost choked, but it proved one
thing: Athletic heroes were still the biggest heroes, and
Nutty had some great days ahead.

That week there was a Student Council meeting,
and Nutty had some trouble getting people to discuss
the issues. Everyone wanted to talk basketball. Nutty was
still trying to keep the pressure on Dr. Dunlop about the
lunches. He had let them have hamburgers a couple of
times—as an experiment, he said—but then he would
forget the whole thing as soon as the meal was over.
Nutty told the students that they needed to pass a reso-
lution, forcing the matter to Dr. Dunlop's attention
again.

It was strange how seriously everyone was taking
him. It was as though he really were somebody now, not
a person you could laugh at. He liked that—even if it
actually made very little sense. That was something else
he told William in one of their many conversations:
"How come I was always just regular ol' Nutty until I
start getting a basketball to go through a hoop?"

William, of course, had thought about that. "Oh,
Nutty, that is one of the great mysteries about our
culture. Men who play boys' games—not engineers—tell
us what kind of car we should drive. And the same people—not nutritionists—tell us what breakfast cereal to
eat. There's no explaining the way people worship athletes."

For the present, Nutty didn't want to explain it. And
that became especially true when Sarah just happened
to be waiting in the hallway when he came out of the
Student Council meeting. He wanted to go over and talk

to her, but he didn't know what to say. As it turned out, however, that was the least of his problems.

"Hi, Nutty," she said, stepping up next to him. It was a fine move, considering that Nutty was already pretty well surrounded by his adoring fans.

"Hi, Sarah. How're you doing?"

"Nutty, you're so cool. I can't believe it."

Cool? He had only said . . .

"How many points are you going to get this week?"

"I don't know. I don't go for points necessarily. If a lot of guys guard me, I pass off."

"It takes a lot of guys to guard you though, doesn't it?"

Sarah was walking slowly, and she changed Nutty's pace. The other kids split off, and the next thing he knew he was alone with her.

Nutty wasn't about to answer her question. He tried to change the subject, making some comment about the lunch problem. But Sarah persisted.

"My dad says you're going to be a pro basketball player someday."

"Well, I don't know." On Saturday, after the game, he was thinking he didn't want to play at all anymore, and now, suddenly, he was thinking he wanted to play for the Lakers or the Celtics, or maybe some team closer to home.

"I'll bet you can make it."

"I'll have to grow quite a bit."

"You're tall now. You'll probably be over six feet."

"Yeah, but you have to be six-five or so to make it these days, even at guard."

"My dad said you can shoot so well, you'll make it no matter what height you are."

"Well, you know—maybe." He felt his face get hot, even as he felt himself switching into his "cool" walk, with his head bobbing ever so slightly.

"Are you just as good at other sports?"

Nutty hadn't thought of that. He probably was. He could probably swing a little baseball in front of his eyes, and then go out there and knock the cover off the ball, and field ground balls like . . . "Well, so far, basketball is my main sport. But I like baseball, and I may play some football in high school. I may even want to consider the major leagues in baseball instead of the NBA. It's still pretty early to say right now."

Geez, Nutty thought, what am I talking about? Last year I struck out four times in one game. If she knew anything about my sports career before . . .

"I don't know. I like basketball better myself. I just think that's what you ought to do. My dad says you're a natural. You know what else he told me?"

"What?"

"I better not tell you. It's too embarrassing."

"Come on. Tell me."

"No. I can't. I never should have brought it up."

"Come on, tell me. You've got me curious now."

They had just arrived at the glass doors at the front of the building. Nutty thought he probably ought to open the door for her, but he didn't, so they each opened their own.

"Okay. But this is just something my dad said. I'm just telling you because . . . well, anyway, this wasn't my idea." She really did seem sort of self-conscious, but she was also giving him lots of those dimply little smiles she had been throwing around every time she saw him lately.

"Okay, okay. Just tell me."

"Well, he said that all the girls were going to be after you, because you were going to be rich and famous and everything. He said I ought to grab onto you while I had the chance." She was blushing bright red, but she was still looking right at him.

Nutty had expected something complimentary, but not quite of that sort. He felt his face heat up about forty degrees, and he couldn't think of one thing to say.

"I mean, you know—he was just kidding. Oh, wow, I can't believe I told you that."

"Yeah, well, uh . . . I don't think . . ."

"See, you shouldn't have made me tell you."

"I don't care if you told me," Nutty said, and then he got out of there.

This was really stupid. Nutty had never felt so weird in his life. His heart was still beating hard and his face was hot—and he wasn't even walking fast. Worst of all, he was wishing he hadn't walked away. He was actually thinking he might like to call her and talk to her some more—but he was too scared to do it.

And so, what he finally decided to do was go over to Orlando's, which was his way of trying to get his mind off all the stuff going around in his head. Or maybe he just wanted to talk to Orlando—or maybe he didn't. He didn't know *what* he wanted.

Orlando was outside, of course. He had his big winter coat on, and he was huffing and puffing, blowing steam around, but he was shooting baskets, as usual.

"Didn't you guys practice in the gym today?" Nutty asked. He hadn't been able to go because of the Student Council meeting.

"Yeah, we practiced."

"And now you're out here in the cold shooting some more. Is that all you ever do?" Nutty said.

Orlando glanced once at Nutty, but he didn't stop. "Yup. I'm going to be better than you again, if it kills me."

"Fat chance. I'm *bad*, man." It was the old challenge, the kind that used to set off a hard game of one-on-one.

"I know. But I'm shooting better all the time."

Nutty lunged forward and knocked a rebound away from Orlando, and then he chased it down, spun, and shot. The ball hit the backboard, a clear miss. Orlando looked surprised. He grabbed the ball and tossed it back to Nutty. "What's with you? You missed one."

"I miss a lot," Nutty said, laughing. He tried another jump shot. It was the old Nutty—the old shot. It banged off the rim.

Orlando was becoming interested. "Okay, let's go," he said. He dribbled away from the basket and then turned to face it, and Nutty picked him up. "Look out, man. Here I come." He dribbled to his right, and then suddenly pivoted, trying to spin around to his left. He lost the ball in the process, but the game was on.

The two of them battled for ten minutes and neither one could hit much of anything. They both tried hot-dog shots, and between-the-legs dribbles, but neither could pull off the moves he was trying. The score was 12 to 8, in favor of Orlando, but they were both so tired they stopped and caught their breaths.

"You're not *bad;* you're just plain bad," Orlando said.

Nutty was laughing. "You're not so great yourself."

"Hey, man, did you see that move I just put on you? I left you standing there."

"You also left the ball behind."

"Yeah, well, I've gotta work some more on that."

Nutty walked over and leaned against Orlando's garage. "Man, I'm beat," he said.

"How come you're doing this?" Orlando said.

"Doing what?"

"Playing like you used to. How come you're not getting those weird eyes and hitting all those jump shots?"

"I just wanted to play basketball, not . . . you know."

"William's making you do something, isn't he?"

"It's no big deal. It's just concentration."

"Don't lie, Nutty. I know William, and I know you. He can always figure stuff out, and you couldn't change that fast if he hadn't done something to you. I think he's hypnotizing you or something like that."

Nutty looked at the ground.

"I don't think it's fair, Nutty. He ought to show the whole team."

"If I show you, can you keep your mouth shut?"

"Yeah."

"What about the rest of the team?"

"Who cares about them?"

Both boys laughed, but when Nutty and Orlando got inside, they made the deal more definite. Nutty would show him what he and William had been doing, but Orlando couldn't tell anyone else.

"Why not?"

"Because William is still experimenting with it. And besides, if everyone finds out about it, maybe everyone will be able to shoot the way I do now."

"Okay, you're right. I won't tell the other guys. But how come you're telling me?"

"I don't know. I shouldn't. I told William I wouldn't."

"Well, never mind about that. Just show me."

"Okay, but it takes some practice."

Nutty found an eraser on Orlando's desk and tied a rubber band to it, and then he told Orlando to lie down on his bed. "Okay, the whole idea is to concentrate, become a sort of machine. The mind knows exactly how hard to shoot a ball, how to aim it and everything. It just has to tell the arm."

For at least half an hour Nutty tried to imitate William's technique. By then Orlando couldn't stand it anymore and had to go outside and try some actual shots. It was getting dark outside, but Orlando didn't care. He made a couple of shots, but he missed a lot more.

"Nutty, that's stupid. That doesn't work at all."

"It takes more practice than that."

Orlando stood looking at Nutty for quite some time. Finally he said, "Are you sure you're not putting me on? I don't see how this could make that much difference."

"I don't know, Orlando. All I know is that it worked for me. Maybe I really am better than you." Nutty grinned at him.

"No way. I'll get the hang of it. I'll be as good as you. And when I am, I'll be better, because I *look* better." He made a couple of shadow moves.

Nutty was laughing, and he was relieved to know that he had shared his secret with someone. But already a certain fear was creeping into his mind. He hoped he hadn't done the wrong thing by showing William's technique to Orlando.

CHAPTER TWELVE

Over the next few weeks Orlando kept trying. Nutty worked with him several times, trying to get him into a trance of concentration. But Orlando was never patient enough; he could never let himself drift into the complete state he needed. He always wanted to run outside and start shooting, and then he would get mad that he couldn't shoot any better than before. At times he seemed to find the groove, the concentration, to pop in some shots. When he did, however, his emotions took over, and that was that.

In the meantime the Labradors won every Saturday morning. That was no problem. They were destroying teams. William had worked out some new designs to get guys open, and with all the double- and triple-teaming on Nutty, someone had to be in the clear. William had read a good deal about defense too, and he was helping the guys improve their basic skills.

Mr. Nutsell had given up all pretense of teaching the game. He let William do all that. He usually didn't even have much to say during time-outs. William took care of that too. But before each game, and during half-time, Mr. Nutsell poured on the lofty speeches as much as ever. He was convinced that William was merely giving the mechanics, that it was he who was moving the team steadily toward greatness by inspiring them with intensity and desire.

While the Labradors were winning every week, so were the Raiders, and whenever the players saw each other, plenty of insults were always exchanged. All this was building for a final game that the players on both teams knew they would have to play—because the two teams had remained tied for first place.

And that's how the regular season ended. A championship game was added to the schedule.

During that last week before the big game, the kids at the lab school really got into the excitement. Even though the league was actually sponsored by City Recreation, not by the schools, Dr. Dunlop allowed the kids to put up some banners in the cafeteria, and a group of girls decided to create their own cheering unit. Not too surprisingly, one of the girls was Sarah.

Sarah saw Nutty in the cafeteria one day that week as he was walking toward his table. Nutty had hardly been able to look at her since the day she had said all those things. And she had been more shy around him too. But he had thought about her plenty, and now he nearly bumped into her.

"Nutty, did you know some of us are going to be cheerleaders for your game this week?" she said.

"Yeah. Someone said something about it, I think."

"Do you mind?"

"No."

"Well, you don't sound too excited about it."

Nutty felt himself getting red again. He hated that. He stood there trying to think of something to say, and then finally came out with, "I think it's neat." Oh, brother! Talk about stupid.

"We don't really have uniforms or anything."

"That doesn't matter." And now he was searching again. "Well, anyway, it's a good idea. I guess I'll see you at the game."

Nutty walked over to the guys and sat down. He was still mad at himself. Why didn't he talk to her a little more? He never got this tongue-tied around anyone else.

The guys were all smiling. "Oh, Nutty, I want to *cheer* for you," Orlando said.

"You're my heee-ro," Richie said.

"Lay off. They're going to be cheering for all of us." The truth was, it made Nutty nervous just to think of Sarah's being at the game.

The guys didn't let up. Nutty had never admitted that he had the slightest interest in Sarah, but they knew—or claimed to. Nutty kept trying to change the subject, and he thought he had done so when he got them talking about the game, but just as they were about to get up from the table, a girl came over to Nutty and asked to talk to him "for a sec." It wasn't Sarah; it was her best friend, Jaimie White.

Nutty set his tray down and said, "Yeah. Sure." He glanced at the guys, and then he said to her, a little more tersely, "What do you want?"

About then Orlando did a resounding "Whoooo-oooooooo."

"Shut up, Orlando. This is Student Council business," Nutty said. But he knew the guys knew better.

Orlando and the other boys cracked up over that, and Nutty's face was suddenly on fire. He walked a few steps away with Jaimie.

"So what do you want?" he said, almost rudely, but he was really embarrassed. The guys were watching, and so were a lot of other people.

"There's something I want to ask you."

"Okay. So ask."

"Well, do you promise you'll tell the truth?"

"Yeah. Just ask, okay?" He glanced over at the guys, who were all grinning. He took a step further away. "Keep your voice down, okay?"

"Okay, but you gotta tell the truth."

Jaimie was always like this. She drove Nutty nuts. "Look, never mind. I've got better things to do than to stand here and—"

"Okay, okay. But answer me honestly. Do you like Sarah?"

"What?"

"You heard me. And you promised you'd tell me the truth."

"None of your business."

"Does that mean you do, but you don't want to say?"

"No."

"Then you don't like her?"

"Why are you asking?"

"Because she likes you."

Nutty glanced over at the table again. He didn't think they had heard, but he told Jaimie to keep her voice down anyway. "Did she say that?"

"Yes. But she doesn't know I'm telling you."

"Well, then, why are you asking?"

"Because she's my best friend. And I just want to know."

"I don't believe that. Anything I say, you'll tell her."

"No I won't."

"Yes you will. I'm not saying anything."

Jaimie rolled her eyes and smiled. "Okay, I'll tell you the truth. She wants to know, but I wasn't supposed to say she liked you unless you said you liked her first. So do you?"

"I'm not going to tell you."

"But that means you do, right?"

Nutty was trying not to smile, but he wasn't doing very well.

"If you don't tell me you like her, I'll tell her you don't like her."

"I didn't say that."

"But that's what I'll do."

"Don't tell her I don't like her."

"Why, because you do?"

"Just don't tell her I don't."

"Then that means you do. That's what I'm going to tell her."

Nutty said nothing; he looked at the guys again.

"Okay. That's what I'm telling her."

"Tell her whatever you want."

"All *right*. That means you *like* her."

Nutty was already walking away, but this last comment had come in squeals—loud enough for half the kids in the cafeteria to hear. Nutty about died. And now he had to put up with a lot more teasing from his friends.

All the same, when he got back to class, he was thinking more about Sarah than he was about being embarrassed. He sort of suspected that the other guys were envious, no matter what they said. Sarah was just about the cutest girl in the school.

But that night, at home, he was a whole lot less thrilled when Susie said to Mom and Dad, "Nutty loves Sarah Montag."

Everyone was in the family room. Dad was reading the paper and trading sections with Mom. Nutty had been watching TV until Susie walked in and made her announcement.

"Shut up, Susie," Nutty said.

"Freddie, don't talk that way," Mom said, but she was laughing. "What makes you say that, Susie?"

"Everyone at school is talking about it. Sarah loves him and he loves her."

"Come on, Susie," Nutty said, "where do you get your information?" He was setting new records for red-in-the-face. He could feel that.

"Today Jaimie White asked Nutty if he liked Sarah, and she told him that Sarah liked him, and Nutty said yeah, he liked Sarah too. Everyone knows about it."

"No, everyone doesn't, because—geez, Susie, you're a pain, you know that?"

She stuck her tongue out at Nutty. "It's true, isn't it?"

"Freddie," Dad said, "is that Martha and Ed Montag's little girl?"

"I don't know." He got up.

"Well, if the daughter is anything like Martha, she's quite a looker."

Nutty was retreating, getting out as fast as he could, even though Mom was saying to him as he left, "Freddie, why are you getting so upset? She *is* a really cute little girl. I know who she is."

Nutty shut the door behind him. "A really cute little girl"—oh, brother. He wanted to crawl under his bed and just stay there—unless Susie came by. She would be worth coming out for. She really had one coming.

But now Dad was knocking and saying, "Son, could I talk to you a second?"

Nutty was still leaning against his door. He took a deep breath, and then he pulled it open. "Dad, Susie is just—"

"Oh, I don't care about that. I wanted to talk to you about something else." But when he came in and sat down on Nutty's bed, he said, "You know how girls are. They can't resist a basketball hero."

"Come on, Dad." Nutty sat down on the floor and leaned against a wall.

"Sorry." Dad laughed, in that high-pitched way of his. "Look, I do have something serious I want to bring up with you. I've been wanting to talk to you about it for quite a while now, but I've been hesitating. I don't want to sound critical, and I certainly don't want to say anything that would change the way you're playing."

"What's the matter?"

"Well, it's about your attitude in basketball . . . and everything else for that matter. You've been awfully cranky lately with your sister, and even with some of the players on our team. And when you play, I've noticed something I don't quite understand."

Nutty had known this was coming sooner or later. Now he wondered what he would say.

"You don't seem to be enjoying the game. You've really taught yourself to concentrate, and you've done just what I've told you to do. I watch you during the games, and I can see you going into yourself. At first I thought that was great, but maybe you're overdoing that sort of thing. You hardly show any emotion at all. If you aren't happy when you make a basket—or when we win—what's the point of playing?"

"I'm happy when we win."

"You don't show it."

"I just don't jump around and stuff. I like to win."

"Do you like the games?"

"Yeah. I guess." But he sounded less than convincing.

"Son, I just don't understand what's going on with you. Most kids would be thrilled to death to be playing the way you are."

"I have to concentrate, Dad. If you don't want me to, then I'll play the way I used to."

"No, no. Don't do that. I certainly don't want you to start playing the way you did in that first game."

"Well, then, I can't help it if I seem sort of strange."

Dad gave that some thought. "Well, for right now," he finally said, "I guess you'd better not change anything. We do want to win."

Nutty wanted to tell him everything. He really wanted to get some advice. But all he said was, "Dad, is it good to get so good that you can't miss?"

"Sure. That's what everyone is trying to do."

Nutty nodded. That was certainly true. And yet, it didn't seem true at all. These days, almost everything seemed that way—true and not true. "You know that stuff you're always telling us, about finding out who we are? What does all that mean?"

Dad looked stunned. "Mean? Well, it means . . . You know what it means."

"Do you just mean to try hard, or do you really mean to understand ourselves? Why do we play games anyway?"

"Son, that's the sort of question William brings up, and I don't think it's worth your—"

"No, Dad. This is just from me. I really don't know why we play sports. Is it really so we'll be good insurance salesmen and stuff like that?"

Mr. Nutsell looked as though a basketball had just bounced off his forehead. "Well, no," he finally said. "It's mainly for the fun of it, I guess."

"Then what's all that stuff about finding out who we are?"

"Well, son . . . it's . . . I guess I mean . . ."

"You know the Pedersons—over on the edge of town? The ones who own the horses?"

"Yes."

"I was thinking about their colts the other day. The young colts run as hard as they can. They kick and jump and run around. It looks like they're doing it just for the heck of it—just to burn up some energy. I got thinking about that, and that seemed kind of nice."

"Nice?"

"Yeah. You know. Like shooting at a basket for the fun of it, and not really caring if you miss a lot of the time."

Dad looked at Nutty curiously and said, "Freddie, I need to think all this over. Is it all right if I . . . talk to you about it at another time?" Then he got up and walked out. Nutty thought he looked confused, maybe even a little worried.

CHAPTER THIRTEEN

All week Nutty wondered whether his dad would bring up their discussion, but he didn't. Nutty thought about it plenty, however, and he had the feeling Dad was thinking too. But it was Saturday morning, just before the family was about to get in the car to go to the big game, before Dad finally said something.

"Freddie, listen," he said, "I think we made things far too complicated the other day." He had come into Nutty's room and shut the door, and he was putting on that old everything's-going-to-be-all-right grin of his. "Sports are for fun. That's the reason for them. But they are also a way to learn about yourself. You learn to win, to lose, to keep trying hard when you're tired—all the kinds of things that can help you in life. And that's why I keep telling you fellows to look inside yourselves. I'm telling you to discover your best self. That's good for the game, but it's also good for anything you do."

This was a little speech, and Nutty knew Dad had worked on it. It wasn't just the stuff that came out of him at practice all the time. But Nutty had thought about all that, and he still had questions. "But what if you have to make a choice, Dad? Is it more important for it to be fun, or more important . . . for all those other reasons you keep talking about?"

"Well, son, I don't see any reason to split the two up. It's fun to do your best. It's fun to win. It's fun to keep trying no matter how tired you are."

Nutty let it go. He almost asked the real question, but he couldn't. Not on the morning of the game. It mattered too much right now to win—both to him and to his dad. If they could win, then he could think about what to do about everything else later.

But when Nutty arrived at the gymnasium, he was unusually nervous. He felt pretty sure that the Labradors could win and that he could shoot well. He was just very aware of certain people who would be there this time. He looked around to see whether the cheerleaders had arrived. He saw no cheerleaders, but he saw some of the Raiders. They weren't being so cocky today, didn't even throw out any insults, but they stared at Nutty with hatred in their eyes.

Nutty wondered why. It was part of what he had been thinking about all week. What was happening? Wasn't it just a basketball game? But when he went into the locker room, his stomach was full of knots.

William was already there. "Nutty," he said, "we need to get you into your trance right away. I don't want all this pre-game stuff to get you all hyped up."

"Naw, come on, William. I don't think I want to. Not yet."

"We can't take any chances today, Nutty. There's a lot more pressure than usual."

Nutty couldn't argue with that. So he and William slipped into a small side room, and William really put Nutty under. He commanded him to forget everything except the game, to feel nothing but the ball, to see nothing but what was on the court.

When Nutty came back into the locker room and began to change, he had never felt more removed from the world. Some of the guys were around, but he didn't even speak to them.

Orlando came over and sat down next to him. "Nutty, I've been practicing hard this week. I think I'm getting it."

"That's good," Nutty said, but the meaning of what Orlando was saying was somewhere outside his head, floating, but never really penetrating.

All during warm-ups Nutty was the same way. He did the drills mechanically, perfectly, and then when he was taking his shots, he hit everything he tried. After the first five or six, the crowd began to *ooh* and *ahh* as each shot split the net, but Nutty knew nothing of that. He liked the feel of the shot, the unity with the ball, the perfection. The game, as it began, was just an extension of the warm-up, simply a chance to have the ball in his hands, to loft it toward the basket.

The only problem was, he couldn't get the ball very often. The Raiders were doing everything they could to keep the ball away from Nutty. Two guys were right with him no matter where he went, and they were especially intent on preventing him from receiving passes from the other players. The first couple of times Orlando tried to pass to Nutty, the ball was stolen, and after that William yelled to forget Nutty for the moment, just to pass off to the other guys.

The Labradors did get some easy baskets, but the guys were kind of tight, and they missed some shots they should have made. The Ridge View team was keeping the score very close. Nutty got off only three shots in the first quarter, which scored, but most of the time he couldn't even get the ball.

Nutty didn't get upset. But he wanted to shoot, wanted everyone to leave him alone so he could arch the ball into the air. He hardly remembered that it was a game with a score, that it mattered who won or lost. He was only vaguely aware that a crowd was there, that a lot of yelling was going on.

In the second quarter the Raiders only became more aggressive. When Nutty got the ball, they practically took his arms off. He was awarded some foul shots that way, which he made, but he didn't get off a single shot from the field. This was beginning to bother him, but it was the fuzzy frustration of a dream—like trying to run when your legs just won't go. He wanted to push these hindrances aside so he could shoot, but he couldn't do that, and so he passed off—or tried to.

And then the guys were off the floor, in the locker room for half-time. Nutty hardly remembered the transition. "Are you all right, son?" Dad was saying. Nutty just nodded.

In the distance somewhere, Dad was soon giving his speech, telling the boys how much the game meant. Nutty felt a sort of longing for that meaning, but he couldn't reach out far enough to grasp it. He was buried in a cloud of heaviness.

William took over, talked about what to do. "Just bring the ball down and play these guys four-on-three the first few times. Nutty, stay way out front and pull two guys with you. The rest of you, cut off the center; someone has to be open all the time. Pass quickly, keep the ball moving, and they can't cover you. Then if they pull back off Nutty, hit him with the ball, and he'll get his shots."

"Stay way out front," Nutty told himself. He could remember that. But he felt something in William's voice, some urgency, and he longed to feel the same thing.

As the boys filed out of the room, Mr. Nutsell took hold of Nutty's arm and held him back. "Son, are you enjoying yourself? Do you really *want* to win?"

"I don't know. I'm . . . concentrating. That's what I do."

"But son, if you don't feel anything, what's the point of playing? All this is supposed to be exciting. Remember what we talked about?"

Nutty felt himself coming up a little, hearing the noise outside. "I know, Dad. But if I get excited, I'll miss my shots."

"Well, I know. But I'd almost rather see you do that than to run around like a zombie."

"What are you saying, Mr. Nutsell?" It was William; he had come up behind them. "Concentration is everything. It's what separates the great players from the good ones. You want the team to win, don't you?"

"Sure I do. But I hate to see Freddie turned into some kind of . . . machine."

"Machines can shoot straighter than humans can, Mr. Nutsell, and computers can make quicker calculations."

"William, go ahead. Go out to the other players. I want to talk to my son for a minute."

"Mr. Nutsell, you'll—"

"Just go, William." For once, Mr. Nutsell spoke with some real authority.

William walked away, shaking his head. But Dad had Nutty by the shoulders, and he was looking straight into his face. "Listen, Freddie, what William just said may be true, but he's wrong. Machines can't feel anything, and that's the best thing about being people—we can."

"But, Dad. People miss. Machines don't. Do you want me to miss?"

"Well . . . no." Suddenly the confusion was back. "I don't know. I want you to play well, but . . . I hate to see you like this."

"I'm okay," Nutty said, and he walked away. But he was feeling something. He was pulling himself up. He had a good look around the gym. The bleachers were packed, and kids were going nuts on both sides. He looked over to the scoreboard at the end of the building. No wonder everyone was so excited. The Labradors were only ahead by three points. He felt something in his stomach, felt his chest tighten; but all this scared him, and suddenly he was pushing it away, letting himself climb back into the safety of his trance. He picked up a ball and rolled it in his hands, felt united with it, and he let himself slide all the way back into the depths.

The second half was frustrating. Nutty stayed outside. He moved around, tried to get open for a pass, but two guys were always with him. It was four-on-three inside, but the three were bigger and quicker, and they were holding up very well against the Labradors. Fortunately, Orlando was playing better than he ever had. He was scoring most of the points, and he was controlling his emotions pretty well. All the same, he was streaky. He would make three or four shots, seem to get excited, then lose his touch and miss everything for a while.

The other guys seemed unusually nervous. Noodle kept dropping the ball or throwing it away. Bilbo was letting the big guys frustrate him. Erin was all over him and was really muscling him out of the way for rebounds.

As the game moved into the fourth quarter nothing had changed. The Labradors would move out to a five- or six-point lead at times, but then they would be back to one or two. They never actually fell behind, but they couldn't break away, either. Nutty had gotten off only four shots in the second half, and he had done that with a hand right in his face on a couple of them. He missed those.

And then the Raiders ran off six straight points and went ahead by two. Mr. Nutsell called time-out. The boys hurried over to the sideline.

"All right, guys, the chips are down," Mr. Nutsell said. "It's all on the line now—our whole season." Then he stepped over to Nutty and pulled him a little to one side. "Freddie, I think it's time for you to wake up. Get excited. We gotta go after 'em."

"Dad, I don't know. I—"

"Well, I do. I want you to have some fun, but I want you to try your hardest. You're not even part of the game."

But William was quick to jump in. "Now listen, fellows." He grabbed Nutty's arm and pulled him back to the group. "Let's try a new strategy. The defenders are expecting Nutty to stay outside. I want you guys to cut off center and then clear to the side, and then, Nutty, I want you to suddenly break to the middle. Give the guys guarding you a fake as though you're moving laterally, the way you have all game, and then just charge to the middle. Noodle, you have to hit him just as he gets clear, so the defense won't have time to adjust."

The guys all agreed and started back out onto the court, but William grabbed Nutty. "Don't listen to your dad." And then in a calm voice, "Just you and the ball. Take it, loft it, let it snap. Your eyes know what to do."

Nutty had noticed the cheerleaders. Sarah was looking right at Nutty, smiling, shouting encouragement. He felt sort of funny for a moment. "Nutty, listen to me. It's only you and the ball. Nothing else is real. Your fingers and your eyes know what to do. Let them take control."

Nutty liked the calmness of William's voice, liked the relaxed way he felt again as he let himself back into the gray quiet.

William's play worked. Nutty broke to the middle, took the pass, pulled up and shot. A perfect arc, and then . . . *swish*. That was good; Nutty knew that. It was making the ball do the right thing. But something else was growing in his consciousness. He wanted to win the game. And with that thought, the noise from the crowd was rising. He moved down the floor, still half in a cloud, but he couldn't resist. He glanced to the side and saw Sarah. She was leaping in the air, excited. Nutty liked that.

Nutty began to play more aggressively on defense. He took the Raiders by surprise, suddenly jumping in and intercepting a pass. And down the floor, the play worked again. Nutty got loose, moving quickly, and he let the ball fly, perfectly, arching, swishing.

He suddenly felt happy. His blood was pumping. He wanted to get these guys. He charged back down the floor, and he heard the crowd going crazy.

CHAPTER FOURTEEN

The next time down the floor the Raiders were looking for the pass in the middle and they closed in quickly. Nutty got the ball and passed off, and Orlando made the shot. The Labradors were up by four and on a roll. Nutty leaped in the air, and yelled, "Way to go, Orlando."

But now the other coach was calling time out. Nutty ran to the side, got there first, and began to slap hands with all the guys as they came off the floor.

"That's what I want to see, son," Dad said.

But William had hold of him. "You're losing it, Nutty. You're going to be on your own if you keep this up. Calm yourself. Think of the ball, the hoop. The ball is everything, Nutty. Think about the ball."

Nutty felt the concentration seep into his head, felt drawn to it in some ways. But there was Sarah, running closer and yelling, "Oh, Nutty, you've got to do it. I know you can."

There was another kind of glow in this, an exciting kind of intensity, that he hated and liked at the same time.

"Nutty, don't do this. I can see it in your eyes. Think of the ball. The ball and the hoop. Break to the middle this time, and if you're covered, drop back quickly. Get the ball. The ball. See the hoop. Don't hear anything. Don't—"

"All right, kids," a ref was saying, "let's get going. We have two minutes, twenty-three seconds on the clock."

Nutty was rattled. All kinds of things were going on in his head. He was grabbing for the concentration that would keep him from feeling, and at the same time looking at the crowd, at Sarah, at his dad—and actually seeing them.

Mr. Nutsell walked out onto the court a little way, and he whispered to Nutty, "Go after 'em, Freddie. This is when you find out what you are."

But William was still there. "Nutty. Just the ball. Think of the ball and the hoop. Get all the rest out of your head."

Nutty ran away from William, and he got tough on defense. So did the rest of the Labradors. Big Erin got off a shot, but he missed, and Bilbo got the rebound. Orlando brought the ball down, and the team cleared the center. Nutty broke to the middle, but that's what the defense was looking for. Nutty pulled up, faded back, and got the pass. He was open. He jumped, got his shot off. "Go in, go in," he yelled right out loud, but the ball hit the back of the rim and bounced off. The Raiders got the rebound.

Relax, Nutty told himself as he ran back down the floor. You're trying too hard. Just relax and take your nice, easy shot.

But the crowd was insane, everyone standing, screaming. And Nutty really wanted to win this thing.

Erin came out front, took the pass, and then bulled his way down the middle, driving for the hoop. Bilbo was right with him, but Erin muscled the ball up, missed, fought off Bilbo for the rebound, and got the ball back up and in.

The crowd was roaring. Mr. Nutsell was screaming at the ref for an offensive foul. The other coach was claiming Bilbo had fouled Erin. And all over the gym, Nutty could hear kids from his school screaming, "Get the ball to Nutty. Take the shot, Nutty."

Relax and concentrate. Just take your time, Nutty was telling himself.

Two guys were on Nutty like a blanket, but William was yelling to the team to slow things down. Pass it around, use up the clock.

With two players covering Nutty, and the rest playing four on three, the Raiders were having a tough time covering everyone; it was fairly easy for the Labradors to keep the ball moving to stall out the clock. Time was ticking away, and finally the Ridge View coach yelled to one of the boys to pull off Nutty and go after the ball.

Nutty immediately broke away from the one player guarding him and took the pass. "Pass it, pass it," William was yelling, but Nutty wanted those two points. He felt great; he was sure he would make it this time. Up he went, and he released a long shot. And it almost went in. It rattled and spun and then flipped out.

Erin grabbed the rebound and tossed the ball down-court to the guy Nutty should have been guarding, and the play went for an easy lay-up. The score was tied.

William was screaming for a time-out.

Nutty walked to the side. He couldn't believe it. What was wrong? He had released the ball just right. He had really thought it was going in.

William was out to meet Nutty. "All right, if you're not going to use my methods, at least don't turn into a gunner. We're going to stall this thing out and try to get the last shot. Orlando, I want you to take the shot."

Nutty was sort of relieved. He didn't want to mess up again. He watched the crowd. The kids on his side were subdued now, disappointed. They were talking back and forth and he knew what they were saying. "Nutty's not so great. He's missing now that the chips are down." Sarah was over there with the other cheerleaders, but they weren't even cheering. She was gnawing on her fingernails, obviously worried. He didn't blame her.

Nutty hated the thought of losing. As he walked onto the court, that was all he could think of. But there was his dad again. "Nutty, get your chin up. Anyone can make a mistake. Go out there and do your best."

"Okay, okay," Nutty said, and he gritted his teeth. This was it.

Richie threw the ball in to Orlando, who passed off to Noodle, who just tossed the ball right back to Orlando. "Twenty seconds," William yelled. He had told Orlando not to make a move to the basket until the time was down to ten seconds. Orlando dribbled to his right, passed off to Nutty, and Nutty passed back to Orlando. "Ten seconds." Orlando dribbled slowly, and then suddenly accelerated into a drive. He was supposed to go to the hoop, hope for a foul, but if he got pressured, pull up and shoot.

But the moment he moved forward, Nutty's man dropped off and double-teamed Orlando. Orlando pulled up, but the guys were all over him. Suddenly he leaped up and flipped the ball back to Nutty. Nutty was open, but he hesitated. And suddenly he was surrounded. He couldn't see anyone. He was twisting, trying to keep the ball away from the defenders, and then he heard William scream, "Shoot now, Nutty. Now!"

Suddenly Nutty leaped up, saw the basket, and tried to snap off that perfect shot of his. The shot was a little too flat, a little too hard, but the ball hit the front of the rim, bounced over to the back, and then back to the front and rolled around. The buzzer sounded, and the ball was hanging, about to fall off.

And then it rolled around and in.

Nutty had been giving it all his body English, screaming for it to drop, and when it did, he leaped straight up in the air. He had hardly come down before he was mobbed. First the players and then the fans were all around him, and he was being hoisted onto somebody's shoulders. Sarah was there, stretching up to him, trying to slap his hand, but she couldn't reach him because everyone else was doing the same. Nutty had never been so happy in his life.

The mob gradually moved to the side of the court. Nutty was trying to get down. "William!" he yelled, and he finally fought his way down and then out of the crowd. He ran to William, who was sitting on the bench, with his arms and legs both crossed. "I did it myself," he said. "That last shot. That was just me."

"Don't I know it. You were lucky it went in." William said something else, but Nutty didn't hear it. He was surrounded by well-wishers again. They were slamming him on the back, telling him how great he was. What had William said?

Suddenly Mr. Nutsell had hold of Nutty. "Son, son. I'm so proud of you. What a clutch shot. You did what you had to do."

"You were right, Dad. You were right. I didn't think you knew what you were talking about."

"What?"

"I mean, I thought all that stuff you kept saying was just—you know—speeches."

It was at least an hour before Nutty got off the court and in and out of the shower. His teammates were whooping it up, and Nutty was loving it. He was right in there with them, as rowdy as anyone.

But William waited, and when everyone else was clearing out, Nutty finally had a chance to say, "What did you say to me out there?"

William leaned back against a locker. "I hate the smell of these rooms," he said, and then he considered for a time. "I said your hero days are over now."

"Why?"

"I think I now understand the flaw in my whole system. It was all too clear there at the end."

"Flaw. What are you talking about? I was great when I used your system."

"Yes, of course. But it requires a certain level of unconcern. The more you care, the more you become a normal human, and normal humans miss. I suspect no one can keep an uncaring distance forever—especially not with females and other such distractions around."

Nutty was suddenly wondering whether a certain female was still waiting out there. "But it's not any fun not to care, William. That's the whole problem."

"Precisely. That's just what I've been thinking about. A person who could make the system work would have to be a machine—as I suggested earlier. But there at the end, when I was screaming and going crazy, I realized that I wouldn't much like any kid—or adult, for that matter—who could be that uncaring."

Nutty laughed. "My dad was right, wasn't he? He was closer to being right than you were."

"Well, I wouldn't go that far. He was usually just—"

"But he always said we were supposed to find out what we can do. If you can't miss, you might as well not play. There's nothing to find out."

William thought about that. "Yes, I suppose so. But your father exaggerates terribly. He gets carried away with all those jock clichés of his. Positive thinking is all fine and good, but really, he makes it sound like—"

But suddenly Mr. Nutsell was pushing his way through the door. "I did it, son," he said. "I took you to the top. I taught you guys to believe in yourselves and now you're champions."

William rolled his eyes, and mumbled something Nutty couldn't hear. Then he chuckled in that grand-fatherly way of his.

But Nutty gave his dad a high five and then a big hug. "You're the greatest coach the Labradors ever had," he said, and Mr. Nutsell seemed to like that very much.

All the same, for some reason, Nutty seemed anx-ious to get away. He slipped past his dad and walked out to the court. A few kids were still around. But Nutty was looking for one particular . . . person. And sure enough, she was still there.

He walked straight over to her. "Sarah," he said, "I've got to tell you something."

She had been about to speak, but now she only nodded, seeming to sense that he was serious. For some reason, she was starting to blush.

"William Bilks taught me how to concentrate so I wouldn't miss any shots, and it worked for a long time. But I don't know whether I can do it anymore or whether I even want to." Nutty hesitated, and she waited to see whether he had something else on his mind. "Will you still like me if I'm not very good at basketball from now on?"

Sarah was deep red by now, and Nutty knew he was too. "Probably not," she said.

Nutty thought she was just teasing. But he wasn't entirely sure. He was sort of nervous, sort of scared, sort of excited, all at the same time. It was the best he had felt in a long time.

"Nutty, you seem to be saying that you think I only like you because you can play basketball. That isn't saying much for me."

"Oh, no. I didn't mean that." Now he was twice as nervous, twice as scared, twice as excited.

He was feeling better all the time.

ABOUT THE AUTHOR

DEAN HUGHES is a native of Ogden, Utah. He received his B.A. in English from Weber State College and his Ph.D. from the University of Washington. After teaching at the university level for eight years, he returned to his home state to pursue a full-time writing career. He also works as a free-lance editor and as a consultant for a firm that presents technical writing workshops.

Among the books he has published for children are a trilogy of novels about the expulsion of the Mormons from Missouri in the 1830s and a further novel about a descendant of one of his earlier characters, as well as modern-day novels: *Nutty for President, Nutty and the Case of the Mastermind Thief, Honestly Myron, Switching Tracks,* and *Millie Willenheimer and the Chestnut Corporation.*

KIDS!
It's Time to Get NUTTY!

☐ NUTTY FOR PRESIDENT
by Dean Hughes   15376-5/$2.50 ($2.95C)

Class clown, Frederick "Nutty" Nutsell and his friends agree: William Bilks is a nurd. But they're in for a big surprise. William is really a genius in disguise, and he is going to prove it by getting Nutty elected the school's first fifth-grade student council president!

☐ NUTTY AND THE CASE OF THE MASTERMIND THIEF
by Dean Hughes   15414-1/$2.50 ($2.95C)

This second *Nutty* book finds Nutty and his friends trying to solve the mystery of who stole the Christmas Fund money from his locker. The school is turned upside down as Nutty and company endeavor to uncover the real—and very surprising—thief!

New! Coming in April!
NUTTY CAN'T MISS
by Dean Hughes

Nutty's father has taken over coaching the school basketball team, and while Mr. Nutsell knows all about school spirit—he knows very little about basketball! Can child genius William Bilks get Nutty out of this one and restore the team's reputation?
On Sale: March 1988.

The long-awaited sequel to *The Chocolate Touch* is finally here!

When John Midas enters a forbidden cave in the Australian Outback, he stumbles into the beginning *of time!*

John Midas thinks this Christmas vacation could be his best ever—the Midas family is bound for Australia! But while his family examines ancient cave paintings, John wanders into the forbidden sacred caves of Ayers, and into a very different world. He finds himself in the Dreamtime, the mythical place where time itself began. Here John must use his twentieth-century knowledge to teach the Australian aborigines the most basic survival skills.

☐ 15567 JOHN MIDAS IN THE DREAMTIME $2.75

☐ 15479 THE CHOCOLATE TOUCH $2.50

THE ENCYCLOPEDIA BROWN WACKY-BUT-TRUE SERIES!
written by Donald J. Sobol. These stories are nutty, wacky . . .
and true! Meet Encyclopedia Brown, also known as Leroy, a
boy with a head full of facts and his eyes and ears on the
world of crime, mystery and intrigue. He's become a best
friend to many, and you'll join the ranks as you read these
funny, fact-filled books.

□ 15358 ENCYCLOPEDIA BROWN'S BOOK OF
WACKY CRIMES $2.25
□ 15497 ENCYCLOPEDIA BROWN'S BOOK OF
WACKY SPORTS $2.50
□ 15346 ENCYCLOPEDIA BROWN'S BOOK OF
WACKY ANIMALS $2.25
□ 15372 ENCYCLOPEDIA BROWN'S THIRD BOOK
OF WEIRD AND WONDERFUL FACTS $2.50

Buy them at your local bookstore or use this handy coupon for ordering:

Bantam Books, Dept. EB2, 414 East Golf Road, Des Plaines, IL 60016

Please send me the books I have checked above. I am enclosing $_____ (please add
$1.50 to cover postage and handling). Send check or money order—no cash or C.O.D.s
please.

Mr/Ms _____

Address _____

City _____ State/Zip _____
EB2—4/88

Please allow four to six weeks for delivery. This offer expires 10/88.
Prices and availability subject to change without notice.

Bant EB2—4/88